CONTRITION

A FALTERING SOULS NOVEL

BOOK 3

BY
HAVEN CAGE

This is a work of fiction. Any similarity between the characters and situations within its pages and places or persons, living or dead, is unintentional and coincidental.

All artwork, on the cover and within this publication, was created by Haven Cage. Stock images used in artwork was purchased from Depositphotos.com and Pixabay.com.

Published by Haven Cage, LLC
United States

I dedicate this story to the lost souls of this world, and the worlds beyond,

To those who've found strength in their faults and the faults of others,

To the people who've fought evil outside, as well as within,
To the hearts that yearn for love and peace while battling the chaos of life,

I dedicate these words to the wary spirits searching for relief at the end of a long, hard road.

In loving memory of the father we lost.
I hope you're happy in the stars.

ACKNOWLEDGMENTS

This is a hard section for me to write. You'd think it would be easy to thank those who've helped you along the way, but after three books in this series, it just seems redundant and very insufficient. I'll never be able to put into words what I feel for the family, friends, fellow-authors, and loyal readers that have stuck with me, book after book. I only hope that I've made you all proud and continue to do so as I advance in the writing world.

Special thanks to:
my husband, my son, and my mother for their endless support,
my grandmother for her constant prayers that this hobby gets me rich one day,
my abundance of wonderfully loyal in-laws, especially my biggest fan #1 and my biggest fan #2. You know who you are...I'll let you two argue over which spot you'll take,
my friends for buying my books and always asking how my book world is spinning, especially Ramah and Paula.

Thanks to Stracey, Janise, and Tracy for regularly posting about me and my books to help spread the word. Your dedication to authors is priceless, and I appreciate all your time and effort.

Thanks to my amazing beta readers—Dina Alexander, Tammy Becraft, Ashley Harley, Michelle Hughes, Cheryl Johnson, Heather Nelson, Diana Quiett, Elizabeth Robbins. Some of you have been with me from the beginning, and some of you have stepped in later, but all of you are a vital part of my books. They would not be what they are without your input and love.

Jaclyn Lee, as my editor, you will always hold a soft spot in my heart. To this day, I believe you are the main influence on my writing. Your guidance and direction has helped me grow so much over the years. Thank you for understanding my mind and helping me translate my worlds into something readers enjoy.

May our burdened souls be released into the glorious folds of peace and rapture when our time comes. May our contrition be enough to carry us to the sky, so we can dance among the stars of eternity.

— Haven Cage —

Wandering Soul

By Haven Cage

Which way will you go?
Toeing the line between guilt and disregard,
I pray it's not too late for my virtue to win, for my soul to return unharmed.

Which way will you go?
Wandering the divide of faith and denial,
I pray you'll turn a blind eye on evil to seek a Holy love, unbridled.

Which way will you go?
Crossing paths of what is correct and wrong,
I pray that Heaven, not Hell, can guide my heart through a life that's troubled and long.

Which way will you go?
Changing lanes on a two-way street,
I pray away my deviant thoughts to make room for those more innocent and sweet.

Which way will you go?
Teetering dangerously from left to right,
I pray that, at the dawn of my time, the Devil will lose this eternal fight.

Which way will you go?
Wavering to and fro,
I pray the Lord can save my faltering soul.

Which way will you go?
Spinning in dizzying circles,
I confess my sins and ask forgiveness of all that is hurtful.

Which way will you go?
Hiding alone in the dark,
I see you trembling there, reaching out to touch the light in my heart.

ARCHARD

HAVEN CAGE

CHAPTER ONE

Behind That Perfect Mask

"No!"

Nevaeh screamed as my flaming blade sliced into Rhett's neck. Black, greasy blood poured from the incision through his throat, coating my sword-like hand. The fire flaring around my blade sputtered for a beat, wavering from a dull glow back to a raging blaze.

There was a soft thump on the dirt when Rhett's head dropped from his body. It tumbled into a double roll before stopping to rest on the high cheekbones of his devilish face, his eyes desolate and empty of life.

Through the flashes of violet lightning sparking from Nevaeh's cloud of doom, I saw her features contort with fear and shock. She kneeled beside Rhett, clutching her pantlegs. She bunched the fabric in tight fists. Her head tipped back while a storm of sin and rage boiled around us.

Her riling hurricane swallowed us up from the rest of the world like a black hole, blotting out any light or life beyond its perimeters. There was no telling what was happening on the outside. Were we surrounded by demons, or had they all fled, taking cover from the war of power happening in their den? And Neveah's parents, their corpses were forgotten in the battle, along with Gavyn's.

As dark as it was folded in Nev's monster's rage, my gaze landed on something far darker billowing out of Rhett's neck. Wicked vapors stretched from the Devil's body and darted straight for my love's mouth, pouring into her with frenzied determination.

Nev choked on the smoggy vapors, her throat stretching to accommodate the abomination fleeing the body beside her.

I allowed my blade to morph back into the flesh and bone of my right hand, the flames dissipating into the dense air. Dropping to my knees in front of Nevaeh, I studied her with caution, unsure of how to help her.

Was this her new gift?

If she was a Soul Bearer, she would be able to harvest souls. Was this part of who she was now?

I tore my eyes from her, focusing on the calming atmosphere. The booming rumbles and electric zaps assaulting my ears hushed. Her storm thinned, the ever-glowing torch lights of Hell penetrating the last wisps of her clouds.

She sat back on her feet and dropped her head. Hair shrouded her face, blocking me from what I wanted to see most—her eyes. I *needed* to see her eyes, *needed* to see if she was still my Nevaeh.

I leaned forward, reaching a trembling hand out to lift her chin. My insides warred with wanting to know who this being was before me and wanting to go on in blissful ignorance.

Her shoulders began to shake, followed by a high-pitched laugh. I paused, my hand an inch from her face. She cackled louder. Her body bounced around the grating sound.

Lowering my hand, I whispered, "Nevaeh?" Her laughter ceased at the sound of my voice. "Nevaeh, are you alright, love?"

She unclenched her fingers from her pants and rubbed slow, wide circles over her thighs. Her breaths came in even, deep pants, but she didn't look up at me.

"Please, look at me, love. I need to see you." My stomach knotted with unease.

"Why?" she whispered back. "Why do you want to see me? What if you don't like who you see?" She chuckled again, stilling her palms. "I'm not the same person I was before, Archard."

2

I combed my fingers through the front of her hair and tucked one side behind her ear. "Look at me," I urged, dragging a finger under her jaw and gently pushing upward.

Her face tilted up a minute amount, enough for me to notice a golden shimmer under her skin. The faint glow rode her veins like a river filling the valleys between mountains.

I ducked my head down to see her better. "Open your eyes, love."

She smirked, raising her face to the skin-patched dome of this horrid section of Hell, her eyes still closed.

Just open your eyes. Let me see who waits behind that perfect mask, I prayed silently.

She flicked her soft tongue over her bottom lip then slowly rolled her head to the right. Her dark curtain of hair shifted to the side, giving me a clearer view of her face. I tensed with the anticipation of meeting the savage Nevaeh had become.

Her thick lashes fluttered open and blinked lazily.

My breath hitched.

Staring back at me were the same lavender-blue eyes I remembered, yet they were different now. She smiled, her lips pulling tight over her pearly teeth. "Not what you expected?"

I squinted at Nevaeh. Squiggles of pale neon-blue and amethyst zig-zagged in circles around her pupils as if her irises carried an electrical current.

"What's happened to you?" I exhaled.

She rolled her eyes and pushed off the blood-caked dirt, dusting remnants of soil and death from her pants.

"I guess, what was supposed to happen," she answered, resting her hands on her hips. She rotated in a slow circle. Her gaze swept over the lifeless bodies scattered around the cavernous room, stopping on Gavyn's. A grin spread across her lips before she marched over to squat beside him.

The Holiness that Nevaeh's grandmother, Theora, had come from the heavens to restore to me was fading fast. I could barely make out what

Nev said, but I managed to detect her mumble with my heightened hearing.

"Good luck, Gavyn. You served me well, now you'll reap the benefits." She smiled, baring her teeth at him, and yanked the blood-splattered gemstone pendant from his neck. Tucking the stone in her back pocket, she popped up and turned to me. "You ready to get out of here?"

I observed her for a moment, considering her mannerisms, the pitch in her voice, and the glimmering streams of gold highlighting the rivers of life under her skin.

Was this really...*my* Nevaeh?

She moved like her, sounded like her.

But...there was something foreign in the spark of her eye. A territory that no longer felt like the soul I'd been bound to when she was born.

I nodded my head. "I think I have enough Heavenly juice to get us out—"

Nevaeh held out her hand to stop my proposal and shook her head. "Don't bother. I've got us covered."

She snapped her fingers in the air then waved her fist in a large loop, trailing a current of bright amethyst lightning behind it. The heat of her power burned and blistered the atmosphere, melting a hole in the very bowels of Hell as if it were little more than a plastic bag catching fire.

"Comin'?" she asked before stepping into the smoldering ring that led us to the human world.

GAVYN

HAVEN CAGE

CHAPTER TWO

NEW KING

A harsh, humid breath of sulfuric air flooded my lungs. I returned to life with a loud gasp followed by an intense prickling racing through my body, lighting my nerve-endings on fire.

One moment, I had found peace in the loneliness and quiet of my death, the next I'm wrangled back to this terrible place.

I roared in pain. Heaving breaths, I winced and propped myself up on my elbows. Dried blood streaked my shirt. Beneath the cloth, I felt the intense sensation of a pick-axe stabbing my chest.

Leaning on one shaky arm, I used the other to drag the stiff fabric up to my chin. My blurred gaze landed on a gaping slit in my breastbone.

The fissure Archard opened in my heart was threading itself together. Strands of vital muscle stretched and burrowed from one side of the laceration to the other, cinching my organ closed. Fresh blood pumped beneath my ribs, spilling from severed pathways into the open crevices of my chest cavity. As my body healed itself, the veins and arteries mended, controlling the flow and steering the fluid to the rest of me.

Every thought was hi-jacked by the agony of my reanimation. I slammed back against the ground, shouting and cursing.

Minutes later, my body was fully repaired, and the torture subsided. I closed my eyes, letting my limbs relax, thankful the process was done.

Distant screams echoed along the endless tunnels. I glared up at a purple, faded heart tattooed on a panel of skin fixed directly above me, wishing I had some earplugs to drown them out. There was nothing I could do for them. They were paying their dues for a lifetime of bad intentions.

Laying here, in the pit of Hell, I supposed I would do the same. I wasn't sure how or why I was back, but clearly, I was resurrected for a reason. The only conclusion I could think of was Hell wanted its pound of flesh from me.

Sniffling, closer than the damned souls' wails, cut into my thoughts of doom and gloom. I jerked my head toward the sound.

A young boy crouched against one of the many living skins stitched to the domed walls and ceiling. His knees were folded to his chest, and he fisted the hair on both sides of his head as if the action would fasten him to sanity. Little did he know, nothing could keep you sane in this maddening realm.

Not even faith.

"Hey, kid," I rasped.

He continued whimpering and sniveling without acknowledging me.

"Kid," I repeated more forcefully. Groaning, I rolled onto my side and stumbled upward off the ground.

The boy's crying quieted. He scowled at me from between his forearms.

Shuffling closer, I maintained eye contact to gain his trust. I stilled when I noticed the familiar shade of crystal-blue in his irises. The slight slope of his nose and shape of his lips reminded me of Layla, a friend-turned-foe I had dispatched in the human world.

"What's your name?" I took a slow step forward.

His head ticked to the side. He glanced to his left as if someone was sitting beside him. After a moment of silence, he aimed angry eyes in my direction.

"You killed my sister," he spat, drops of spittle spraying his knees. Tears formed in his blood-shot eyes.

He *was* Layla's little brother.

I opened my mouth to apologize but pressed my lips together instead.

8

What good would it do now? No amount of saying sorry would mend his heart. Besides, I wasn't sure I regretted what I had done.

Layla had weaseled her way into my café as an employee, then into my heart as a friend. She wanted more from our relationship, but it never felt right to me, especially not after Nevaeh came into my life.

Layla manipulated me. She tried to change my feelings for Nev. The woman lied to me and used her Dark Celata powers to threaten us. When that didn't work, she black-mailed me into giving up my soul to save Nev from what I thought would be a worse fate.

As it ends up, Nevaeh fell into that dismal fate all by herself anyway, surrendering herself to Hell's clutches to save me and George.

She couldn't save me, though.

That bitch, Layla, used us to better her stature in the Dark Prince's eyes, taking us on missions to damn other human souls under the Devil's will.

My mind had all but fried in the misery, regret, and sorrow of this fucking place.

I found Layla in my apartment, with Nevaeh, attempting to force her to return to Hell. Nevaeh had escaped with George's soul. I may have been on the brink of madness, but I couldn't let Layla interfere with Nev's chance to save herself and to save George.

So, I shot Layla in the head.

Somehow, Nev and I ended back in Hell afterward.

I'd given up nearly every fiber of my faith, every strand of my sanity, trying to make things right, and look where it got me.

Apparently, what I did to Layla, or maybe just returning to the Devil's playground, was my breaking point—my point of no return.

In my dark confusion, I surrendered to the fake promises of retribution and change whispering in my head and forced Nevaeh to kill her parents.

I was the one who coerced her to fulfill a blacker destiny than all of us.

Archard showed up to save her, but it was too late. I'd already forced her hand.

The faint memory of him plunging his blade into me lingered amid my thoughts.

Dropping my gaze to the dirt floor, I swallowed the lump of shame and guilt forming in my throat. I wouldn't take back what I'd done to Layla because she was poison and had it coming—I'd gladly pay my dues for that—but I'd pray for forgiveness every single day of my miserable, returned life for what I'd done to Nevaeh.

Hell was going to have a field day with me. I'd never be allowed to forget my sins.

The kid narrowed his eyes at me, tilting his head to the right a notch. "They say you're not even sorry. Well, you will be. You'll pay heavily for what you've done. They say so." A satisfied smile cracked behind the streams of tears running down his face.

"Who says?" I challenged.

"The voices of Hell chatter in my ear. They are happy to talk to me. So happy that I'm here," he whined.

Lowering his head, he tucked back into the comfort and protection of his arms, tightening trembling hands around clumps of his hair. His sniveling started again.

"Listen, I did what I had to. Your sister was hurting people," I explained.

His muffled voice responded with, "Did that truly give you the right to hurt her? To hurt me?"

Months ago, I would have considered his question with a greater weight. Now, I felt compelled to answer with a quick and absolute, "Yes."

It was right, wasn't it? Hurt those that hurt others? Seek revenge where you can?

I squeezed my eyes shut and pinched the bridge of my nose. The lines of right and wrong had blurred well beyond my capabilities of clarifying as of late.

"What is your name?" I growled, irritated that he was making me doubt my principles. I was so tired of being manipulated. He was just like his sister.

"Dominic," he hiccupped through his whimpers.

"Alright, Dominic," I twisted, scanning the exits out of the skin room, "we need to find a way out." Regardless of how I felt about his sister, he was a young boy who hadn't hurt anyone to my knowledge. I couldn't leave him here.

Hysterical laughter bubbled from his chest. His head slowly lifted, his arms falling to drape across his knees.

"What's so funny?"

His head tilted as if listening to the voices again, but he held my gaze. Dominic barked out another chuckle.

"What?" I yelled, rage boiling in my blood.

"You can't leave," he said. "You're tethered to Hell."

I shook my head. "I know there are demons who can open portals here. We just have to find one, then follow them out...," my words died off when I lifted my hand to touch the stone Layla had used to cross portals. It was around my neck when I woke up after Nev pulled me through with her. Now, it was gone.

"They say the stone wouldn't do you any good anyway."

"Quit being so fucking vague! What are you talking about?" Panic tightened its fist around my heart. "What do you mean, 'tethered?'"

"There's always a balance with good and evil. Your body died down here, the Devil's soul left the confines of this realm, and so, they say someone must take his place. There must always be a balance. Always a balance."

My eyes widened. My stomach dropped. My knees wobbled.

That was why I healed...to assume the reins of Hell?

Dominic chortled, "Told you that you'd pay, didn't I?"

HAVEN CAGE

ARCHARD

CHAPTER THREE

Big Plans

I followed Nevaeh into the abandoned textile factory that we, the other Earth-bound angels and I, called home.

It felt like years since I'd seen my brothers' faces. So much had happened before I'd left the human realm to find Nev and bring her back. They had no idea about Arkin, Arianna, Malach, and I finding the Clavis Prophecy and the Key, or Nevaeh's dead grandmother, Theora, descending from Heaven to return some of my Holiness.

Though I'm sure my second hand and best friend, Arkin, filled them in on what he knew before I left, none of them would have a clue as to what went on in Hell. As far as they knew, if I came back with her, she'd be the Nevaeh they had learned to love and respect from the beginning of this mess.

Staring at the dark, tangled curls swaying down Nevaeh's back, I wondered if it was her that I'd invited here, or something else entirely.

The tips of her hair were starting to fade, the rich brown hues draining to an ashen white. It made me think of the color staining the tips of my wings, and the wings of my brothers, from losing our Holiness. It was the stain of sin and abandonment, a constant reminder of how far we were from God.

Was this Nevaeh's soiled soul leaving its external mark for the world to see?

She stopped in the hall leading to the large training room. We'd barely said a word to each other during our journey here from the outer city limits. What was there to say? It seemed words could not rectify anything that had happened since she left us.

"You okay?" I probed.

She nodded her head. Her shoulders slumped for a moment, then she straightened her back and lifted her chin.

Just as I reached to touch her arm, she stepped forward. I curled my fingers anxiously, eager to feel her skin, to feel our connection.

She pushed the steel door open and entered the room where she'd seen the angels last.

A hush fell over the Guardians. Each one stopped what they were doing as if someone had flipped their off switches at the same time. Their gleaming eyes trailed Nevaeh's movements deeper into the cavernous room until she stood in the center of them all.

The slender woman with electric purple eyes and graying hair spun slowly, meeting every warrior's gaze. They observed her with curiosity and trepidation.

Perhaps my brothers could sense the change in her as keenly as I had.

Perhaps they saw something I'd missed in the blindness of love.

Footsteps scuffled from the back of the room, then Arkin pushed through the crowd. "Get out of my way, you ogres." His eyes landed on Nevaeh, and he stilled. "Sweet-cheeks," he exhaled with a hint of relief.

Nevaeh peeked over her shoulder at me, the glint of violet shining in her irises.

Arkin barreled into her, encircling her small body in his thick arms like a toddler trying to hug a reluctant kitten. She wiggled in his grip, but soon relaxed and let him squeeze the air out of her.

"It's been too long. Don't ever leave us again," Arkin ordered.

"Oh, I don't plan on it," Nevaeh assured.

When Arkin stepped back and allowed her some space, the other angels lowered to one knee, genuflecting before Nev.

I paced around the crowd, scrutinizing Nevaeh's reaction. The lines in her face, the creases of her pleased expression, it all seemed to be her, but not completely.

She approached Amil, the closest to her, and brushed a finger down his cheek. He beamed up at her for a second, joy and respect in his gaze, then lowered his head. "Welcome home, Clavis."

Nev made her way to every Guardian, accepting their salutations like tithes. Once she finished, she held up her hands, gesturing for them to stand. "Rise, my angels. You are my brothers, now. I'll need your help to win this war, to make the world what it should be."

They thrust up, ruffling their wings and murmuring collectively in agreement.

Arkin's eyes darted to me. His brow pinched together. The same question seemed to linger in his mind as did mine.

Was she the real Nevaeh?

I gave a half shrug and rubbed the tense knot of uncertainty forming on the back of my neck.

We would have to watch her for now. Hopefully, her actions would show us who she really was. I just prayed it wouldn't be too late if we were wrong.

Nevaeh sauntered toward me, yawning. "I'd like to get some rest before we make our next move."

"And what move would that be?"

Her lips curled into a sly smile. "Fulfilling my destiny, of course," she chimed like I was silly for even asking.

Neveah turned to leave, but I wrapped my needy fingers around her bicep and tugged. "Don't you think you've done enough destiny fulfilling for a while? You just lost your parents...your friend." I averted my gaze to avoid eye contact.

I'd killed someone who was a good man before the poison of wickedness took over his soul. Gavyn could have been Nev's future, and I took that away from her.

Yanking her arm from my grasp, she faced me and stepped in close, forcing me to look at her. "I *murdered* my parents, Archard. I didn't just lose them in the woods somewhere. And *you killed* the one decent man I'd met aside from George. We have to live with that, now." Her expression was stone-cold.

She bit into her lower lip, letting it slide along the edge of her teeth as she bridled her anger. "While we deal with the facts that we are killers, there is a world begging to be molded into something greater. I was given a gift. I'll be damned if I let it go to waste because I'm wallowing about a past I can't change. I've been given a second chance, I'm going to make the best of it. I'd appreciate any help you can spare to give me, if you're not too busy judging and crying about your indiscretions."

Just like that, her fierce, fiery disposition transformed to a grinning vixen. "You look like shit. Wanna come rest with me?" she asked in the sultry voice I longed to hear every second she was away.

I crossed my arms and shook my head. Something didn't feel right. *She* didn't feel right. There was a sick itch in my gut and a dull ringing in my ears. "I'm going to stay here and catch up with my brothers." I winked and smiled as genuinely as possible. "Get some sleep, love."

"Ok, but, when I get up, I've got big plans."

ARKIN

HAVEN CAGE

CHAPTER FOUR

Dust Off The Old Prayer Box

Archard paced the floor, shoving his hands through his long blonde hair. "I don't know what the hell to think, Arkin."

"Well...Malach said she swallowed Layla's and Father Varga's souls at Gavyn's, right? He seemed pretty convinced she had her head in the right place then. Maybe, she's just recovering from everything that's happened. She's been through a lot, Archard. Give her time."

He faltered in the middle of my room and fell to his knees. His back bowed under the relentless weight of grief and uncertainty. He curled in on himself.

"You didn't see it," he whispered through streaming tears. "It was so dark. Her rage was as thick and sharp as a briar patch of thorns. Then, whatever came out of Rhett..." He inclined his head to the ceiling, breathing heavily. "There's no way that evil couldn't have pushed her over the edge."

His cloudy gaze shifted to me, searching for a promise that she'd be okay. I couldn't give it to him.

"I feel it too, man. She's different. I can't put my finger on it, but I feel it in the air around her."

He didn't move or respond to my admission.

I jammed my hands in my pockets and cleared the worry from my throat. "What do you want to do? Do you want to lock her up or something?" I kept the tone in my words as calm as possible while hoping he'd come up with a better solution. I wasn't sure I could cage Nevaeh like a rabid animal.

With slow, heavy movements, Archard schlepped himself off the ground. One of his hands curled around the back of his neck and squeezed. "No," he exhaled. "Just watch her. Have some of the others follow her if she leaves."

His eyes searched the ceiling, a reflex we all have when we are seeking His help. "I feel like she's a stranger. I know her, Arkin...deeper than I know myself." He shook his head, his aqua eyes lowering to me. "Why does she feel so damn far away?"

The anguish in his voice was beyond heart-breaking. I had no idea how to answer that.

"Maggie will be here soon. Maybe she can spend time with Nevaeh and give us some peace of mind."

Archard trudged closer and placed a hand on my shoulder. "Thank you, brother."

I forced my lips into a weak smile and nodded.

After he left, I fell to my knees and prayed.

It wasn't something I did often anymore, but I felt like this was a good time to kick the dust off the old prayer box I kept shoved into the corner of my brain.

I asked for forgiveness. I begged for help.

I prayed for salvation from whatever was to come.

MAGGIE

HAVEN CAGE

CHAPTER FIVE

A DULL GLOW

She looked so peaceful, lying on the mattress on Archard's bedroom floor. Nevaeh's long, hickory-hued hair undulated in curls around her slack face and cascaded across a white pillow case where the bleached tips of her locks blended with the fabric.

A soft, rhythmic inspiration and expiration of air was the only sound in the room. Her serene breathing was a far contrast to the chaos I felt radiating off her body while she slept.

I leaned into the doorjamb, nibbling on my already non-existent thumbnail, and observed the woman who jump-started the self-destructing world we lived in now.

A mass of colors—blazing red, emerald green, powder blue, and a shameful gray—floated around her like a dark soap-bubble. No...floated wasn't the right word. They twisted and snaked, weaving over and under each other in a tangled blanket of rage, jealousy, righteousness, and guilt. Beneath that was a dull glow of hope and determination, barely a flickering flame next to the riling torrent of colors fighting for dominance cocooning her.

It had been hours since Arkin called me, but, due to an issue with a missing Celata I'd agreed to help with, I couldn't leave right away. It was better this way, though, seeing her at her most vulnerable.

After our last meeting at the club on Queens, when I witnessed her black globe of fury swallowing a man while Layla tried to kill me, I wasn't naïve enough to put a limit on what her powers could do. And she was much stronger now.

Resting my temple against the wood framing, I stared hard at her cast bubble. I wondered which of the colors was truly Nevaeh and which was one of the souls she'd eaten. How long before one of the others' energy overtook her poor spirit and devoured Nevaeh from the inside like a parasite?

Even a Celata with rare gifts and half-demon blood couldn't possibly harvest souls and carry them for longer than a few weeks. Could she? I'm sure a true Soul Bearer couldn't let the souls ride them that long without some sort of side-effect, and they were made for it.

I rolled my eyes at myself. I was being stupid. I had no idea how a Soul Bearer worked. Who was I to assume anything?

With everything happening so fast—Malach finding Nevaeh nearly defeated by Gavyn and Layla, her harvesting the souls at Gavyn's before crossing back into Hell, and Archard receiving his Holiness back to chase her—we hadn't been able to sit down and have a good pow-wow yet. There was still too much info missing for me to make assumptions.

Tearing my gaze away from the swirling colors hovering around Nevaeh, I glanced at my leather boots and wished I had more definitive evidence to give Archard. At this time, there was no telling how the last few days had affected her, or what her future intentions were.

"It's rude to watch a stranger sleep."

I flinched, snapping my head up to see Nevaeh's violet eyes studying me. "I'm sorry. Archard asked me to check on you."

She threw her legs over the edge of the bed, sitting up to see me better. Her head rolled in a slow circle, stretching from her nap. "What's your name?"

"Maggie."

"Well, come in, Maggie. I promise I'll behave," she purred with a sweet smile.

The impish tone behind her words and the flicker of lightning in her eyes led me to believe she was anything but sweet.

"I'm good here, thanks." I pushed off the door frame, stiffening my posture to portray confidence.

Her gaze raked over every inch of me with curiosity, then she narrowed her eyes. "Have we met before?"

I nodded. "In the alley…beside Cravings on Queens."

Tilting her head a tick, she slanted her eyes to the left as if sifting through old memories in her mind. Her face suddenly lit up, and she regarded me with recognition. "That's right. I thought you were a goner."

"Nope. I'm made of tougher hide, I guess."

Nevaeh rose from the bed, chuckling. "I guess so," she said, taking a step toward me.

God help me, I took a step toward her as well. Something about her drew me in like a magnet. No, she was a bug-zapper, and I was the stupid mosquito headed straight for her pretty, deceiving light.

She inhaled a deep breath and opened her mouth to speak, but paused, pinching her brows together. "Relax, Maggie. I'm not gonna hurt you."

Fighting her pull, I eased to my right and pretended to inspect a crack in the wall. "I'm not afraid of you hurting me, Nevaeh."

"You're so tense. Look at you, all stiff and distant." She slinked toward me.

I shrugged a shoulder, shaking my head. "I'm always like this. I just don't trust people I don't know. You're no different."

She stopped abruptly and clasped her hands over her chest like I'd broken her heart. "Oh, aren't we the pair? I'm the same, Maggie." Her gaze bore into me, reaching for my secrets. "I'd like to gain your trust, though. I don't have a lot of friends, and I could use a few good souls on my side." Closing the gap between us, Nevaeh opened her arms and latched onto me. A low, cheerful sigh blew over my shoulder. "See, isn't this nice? We could be besties before the week is out," she said, hugging me tighter.

My body relaxed into her hold.

It *was* nice.

Maybe her intentions weren't so bad.

Maybe she just needed to adjust.

Maybe we *could* be best friends.

I've always wanted a woman to bounce my ideas off, complain to, and do girlie stuff with. It would be nice to share this crazy life with a friend who knew what it was like to be a Celata.

My hands lifted to her back. I closed my eyes, breathing in her spiced lavender scent, and sank happily into her embrace.

Or maybe this was all some ploy to manipulate us

NEVAEH

HAVEN CAGE

CONFESSION OF A LOST SOUL

Can you hear me?

Can *anybody* hear me out there?

Guess I'll just talk and pray that you are listening.

Listen very carefully to every word I'm about to tell you. Before he comes for you too.

I'm not sure what makes me think you'll be able to get my message, but I have to believe maybe I can save a few of you, if you are sensitive enough to know me, I mean really know who I am at the core.

God, I don't even know where to begin, now.

It's so hard to think in here. I can hear *him* talking, but I can't do a damn thing to stop it.

Well, if you know who I am, you've likely been with me through the entire ride — since I opened my eyes to this crazy, dangerous world. Use my mistakes as a guide to steer clear of him. Don't try to be the hero...it never works.

How could I have been so stupid?

There was a time I thought life could be worse. Why harp about sleeping on the littered, wet cement with a blanket wrapped around my shoulders and day-old bread from a restaurant down the block in my stomach? Most of the world lived with incurable diseases, contaminated water, and days full of loneliness and regret.

I had George, ya know? I had small mementos of my past. Though I couldn't remember much of my childhood, my mother's locket and the blanket my grandmother made me showed I was loved. I had enough food to keep me alive. That should have been enough, right?

I had no right to want for more than I'd been given.

What made *me* so special? That's what I kept asking myself.

Unfortunately, I was right.

Life could be worse. Do you hear me out there? Much fucking worse.

It could be complete Hell, literally. If humans were aware — truly cognizant — of where their souls could end up after they died, the world would be full of loving, caring people. Some, because of faith. Some, because of the purest and deepest fear.

Maybe that's the reason for all this.

I don't know.

Grr. It seems like I've spent years in here already, trying to figure it all out. I've poured over every step I took, wondering which ones weakened my tight-rope that much more, until there was nothing left to keep me from falling. I scoured all the missed opportunities that could've changed everyone's lives for the better.

In the end, I realized it didn't matter. I fucked up. There is nothing I can do to go back and fix the shit-storm I've made. I doubt I'll get the chance to express proper contrition for all that I've done.

Had I known, I would have been a believer from the moment I learned the truth. I would have been on my knees every day afterward, praying to a higher-being and counting the days until I could feel that majestic embrace — had I known.

Oh, what I'd give to feel that all-encompassing warmth on my soul. There's just a dank chill that freezes my nerves, skimming up and down my spine like a spider weaving a never-ending web.

My stubborn soul allowed doubt to needle into its core, cracking me with pressure from the inside out. My demonic side latched its claws around my heart and refused to let go, which I thought might be the key to my freedom, but now I'm not so sure.

Gavyn sacrificed his faith for me and lost his mind — and life — in the process. Layla played my friend to dig her bloody hands into Gavyn and did everything in her power to make my life harder. She died as well. I still feel her, though. She's in here with me...somewhere.

George is in here too, emitting a subtle drone of energy. He's the only comfort I feel in this desolate wasteland.

After I harvested his soul, along with Layla and Father Varga, the priest, I could hear them, sense their intentions, feel their essence in my mind, livening my body.

Those sensations were quieted in the blink of an eye, overpowered by an eternally damned phantom I can't shake.

I walked right into his trap, killing my parents and completing some fucked-up ceremony to awaken the new power flowing in my veins.

I'm not sure what I gained when the bloody ink on the Clavis's pages mixed with my parents' life-essence and soaked into my pores, but I'm sure I'll find out soon enough. I have a feeling it won't be good either.

He planned this all along.

Bron...or Rhett...I don't even know what the fuck to call him. Perhaps, The Devil is the only title I need to use in his reference.

That's what he is, right? The Leader of Demons?

From flashes of memories that seep into my mind, I know he's not the first Devil to reign over the Underworld, but he's the one I have to deal with now. He's the angel-turned-demon that has managed to lock me away inside myself.

He is the malevolent soul slowly suffocating me with my own darkness.

It's so strange. I'm aware of myself and my form like a distant glimmer in the back of my mind, but I can't gain control of anything I do.

Don't fall prey to his deceit. Don't be blinded by whatever he does in my name.

It's not me.

If you can hear me, please, tell Archard I'm in here.

Tell him...I'll never give up.

HAVEN CAGE

MALACH

HAVEN CAGE

CHAPTER SIX

Disruption Of Balance

Bursting through the watery portal, I flew upward then softened my knees for landing. Once my feet flattened against the grassy floor of Heaven, I tucked my wings against my back and smiled.

Coming home always filled my body with exhilaration and my veins with a buzzing flush of power.

I inhaled, appreciating the atmosphere, letting the molecules of Holy space and time flow through my cells. The air here felt lighter, free of pollutants...the purest form of breath.

For the life of me, I couldn't figure out how I could ever forget such a place, but the more time I spent on Earth, the more memories and sensations of this place slipped from my senses.

I peered up at the spectrum of majestic colors waving across a black velvety sky like the Northern Lights in Alaska. Bright specks of white light flickered through the ribbons of bold ruby, sapphire, turquoise, and emerald hues. Outer space was the closest thing to Heaven humans knew during their Earthly lives, but even the marvels of the universe paled in comparison to my home.

Each flash of the distant orbs warmed my heart. They were the reason we fought this war with the demons. I knew I sometimes forgot the importance of human life, but returning home and seeing the endless spirits who devoted themselves to living a good life, restored my faith in humanity.

My gaze lowered to the iridescent gateway in front of me. A beautiful white glow radiated from behind the gate, bleeding God's Glory into the dark sky like city lights seen from the countryside.

The gate guarded the three spheres of our realm. Each sphere segregated us, angels, by our duties and responsibilities. Our hierarchy and existence depended on what part of Heaven each of us were born to serve.

Archangels, Principalities, and lesser angels, like Guardians, lived closest to the Human realm in the third sphere. We carried out orders regarding humans. The second sphere housed the Dominions, Powers, and Virtues. They were given more power and jurisdiction than the third sphere angels, governing those beneath them. They also dealt with governing the cosmos, time, and nature. Seraphim, Cherubim, and Thrones occupied the first sphere, closest to God. They were gifted with the Holiest of duties and tended to the Lord's needs.

Sometimes, situations called for us to be assigned new responsibilities, such as my becoming a Guardian, but there was always a balance to be kept among the ranks.

The separate spheres also created a buffer from the intensity of Father's power. Not all of us were made to stand so close to the flame.

I examined the four delicate, evenly spaced, spindles tapering from six feet to eight feet above my head. Shimmering rods swirled in fluid loops and curves, ending in intricate flourishes to create two richly adorned gates fit for a king.

Fences, mimicking the same elegant patterns, stretched in either direction, appearing as if they ended ten yards out. Clear meadow landscape reached out beyond that, giving the impression that someone could walk around the end and enter the Holy Kingdom. I knew that if someone were to walk to the edge of the fence, though, they would find themselves at the beginning of another ten yards of shining barricades.

No human essence entered Heaven without the Soul Bearer's help. They were the gatekeepers of Heaven and the deliverers of Hell. Angels could walk through, but only under certain circumstances.

The third-sphere angels could pass through more easily since they had direct interaction with the Human realm, but even they must have purity and righteousness in their soul. Otherwise, the bars did not budge.

I trudged forward, swallowing the lump of sadness and fear gathering in my throat. Reaching a hand out, I skimmed the structure floating at eye-level in front of the entrance to Heaven. It resembled a large urn flipped upside down.

My fingers traced along the slender neck at the top and slipped downward along the smooth, marbled surface until they encircled the wide rim at the bottom. A rough edge on the back bit into my skin, drawing blood from my fingertip.

There was a crack in the vessel.

My hand dropped, shaking from what a crack in the Soul Transcender meant.

After a spirit was collected by the Soul Bearer, they returned and placed it in the Transcender. Somehow the soul was transferred from the vessel to the haven above, becoming one of the orbs shining in the safety of God's prismatic fold. There, the soul enjoyed its own version of Heaven—its own personalized world of happiness and bliss. Often, if people's happiness were connected on Earth, their worlds reconnected in the afterlife.

I ducked, looking North through the open ends of the Transcender, and choked on a gasp. What usually offered a detailed window into any given orb, was black now. It was as if someone put the lens cap back on the telescope.

Suppose we could get Nevaeh to reap the souls from Earth and act as the new Bearer, the cracked vessel may be of no use. She wouldn't be able to transport them to their proper places. And, what was worse, I wasn't sure there was any way to fix it. This was unheard of. It's not like we had a back-up Transcender on standby.

Straightening, I smoothed my hand over the vessel one last time then marched toward the gates. I lowered to one knee and let the faith I held in my heart ring loud from my center. It was a gesture all angels performed to seek permission to proceed.

The doors remained closed.

"It's no use."

I spun on my knee and lunged upward, drawing my sword from its sheath, ready to defend. I halted with the tip of my blade centimeters from her throat. Long, brown curls and eyes matching Nevaeh's flipped my switch of recognition. "Theora?" Relaxing my stance, I lowered my weapon.

"I can't figure out how to get back in." Her dainty chin motioned to the barrier behind me.

She held fistfuls of her floor-sweeping gown up against her thighs, so she wouldn't trip when she moved closer.

Her radiance when she came to the human realm to restore Archard's Holiness was nothing next to the pure illumination she carried in this realm. Her flawless skin and silky hair bestowed such a beauty, it was hard to look directly at her.

As Nevaeh's grandmother and Arkin's ward, I'd heard a few stories about what a powerful Celata Theora was. She'd kept Nevaeh safe well into her old age, but her house was eventually overrun with demons.

When she tried to escape with Nevaeh, she lost her life. Her last request was for Archard and Arkin to relinquish their Holiness, so they could be Earth-bound and fight for her granddaughter.

Theora's devotion seemed to have paid off. She ascended to sainthood in her afterlife.

"Have you been outside the gates since you returned from the human realm?" I asked, confused about why we couldn't get in.

She stopped next to the Transcender, cutting a sad side-glance at it, and nodded. Her eyes met mine, weariness darkening their clear blue depths. "I walked the fence for a while, calling out to anyone who might be able to hear me. When no one came, I decided to venture away from here. I thought maybe others were stuck outside like me. Then, I considered that perhaps I was being punished for giving Archard back his power." Theora bowed her head.

"No. I don't believe that." I marched to the glimmering bars, grabbing hold to shake them loose. They didn't budge.

"I already tried that, Malach."

"Why didn't you come back and tell us?"

Shaking her head, she said, "I gave him every last bit of my Holiness, except for just enough to get home. I have nothing left."

Huffing out a breath, I slid to the ground and leaned against the gate, soaking up the hum its divinity vibrated into my spine.

My gaze wandered to one of the many flumes of wispy clouds scattered around Heaven. The same wondrous colors that rippled above played among these lower vapor-collections, decorating the angels' level as well.

"Did they make it back?" Theora whispered, lowering to a spot next to me. She crossed her legs and leaned back, waiting patiently for my answer.

"Yeah. I got message that they had just before coming here." I said, tearing my eyes away from the rolling cloud to look at her. "They wouldn't have without you."

Theora smiled appreciatively, but it didn't last. She stared down at her fingers clasped in her lap. Her right thumb rubbed a soothing circle over her left thumb. "I'm sure they would've found another way."

I opened my mouth to tell her she was wrong. A loud slap against the bars behind me erased my train of thought.

Theora and I scrambled away from the barrier. Our eyes focused on the panting angel laying at the foot of the gate with his battered fingers wrapped around a spindle.

"Oh, Lord!" Theora shrieked. Her hand flew up to cover her mouth. She stiffened with fear and surprise.

Kneeling on the ground, I reached through the bars and brushed a lock of blood-matted hair from the angel's face. Based on the thin strip of silvery light wavering under his forehead's skin like a mercury crown, and the simple platinum scepter fastened between his narrow smoke-hued wings, he was a Principality.

His kind could transform from a fully human form to a completely translucent spiritual form in the blink of an eye. I'd only met a few since my creation, having to work side by side with them in matters of the human realm during past near-apocalyptic events.

Normally, they hovered around large cities, following orders from the higher-up angels to keep nations thriving as well as possible without breaking the Heavenly rules of interaction.

I slapped his face lightly. "Hey, man. Hey, wake up."

The tattered angel's body shifted from solid to an ethereal mass similar to the floating rainbow-clouds wandering around us.

"Wait...stay with us," I shouted, trying to grip some part that wasn't fading to air. My fingers drifted through him.

Theora crawled next to me and reached through the spindles, gliding her hand over his outline. "Come back to us, Ravlon."

Sitting back on my heels, I perched my hands on my thighs and watched her soft manner coax the damaged being back to us.

Once his contours returned to a more tangible state, he roused, groaning under Theora's touch. "They broke the chain," Ravlon rasped.

I leaned in, wrapping my fingers around a pearlescent spindle. "Who broke what chain?"

"The Dominions. They broke the chain of angelic spheres," he croaked.

Theora's gaze whipped to mine, worry lines creasing her forehead.

She knew what that meant as well as I did.

The Dominions were a governing cast. They regulated the commands of God, issuing duties to the lower-sphere angels who dealt with the Earthly realm directly. If they broke away from God's ranking, the lower angels didn't have Heavenly guidance. They couldn't know what was best for humans based on God's great plan.

Beyond that troubling reality, the Lord was essentially being held hostage with the higher casts. He was a prisoner of His own power.

There was a reason we had so many ranks; God's power was too consuming to interact with humans directly. He could destroy them all without meaning to. That was the cause of him taking different forms...Jesus Christ...The Heavenly Spirit. Now, they were all trapped. We were his armor...the humans' armor.

"Ravlon, can you tell me what happened in there?" I barked, trying to wake him from his stupor.

"They tricked some of the third-sphere beings to assist them in the betrayal. Ordered them to kill anyone who stood against them. Said we were the betrayers. I fought...we all fought...once we knew, but it was too late." He sputtered around a weak cough. "They overthrew us."

"Where is everyone else?"

"Mending however they can." Blood bubbled from the corner of his mouth. "I...I made it here...hoping to reach those on Earth. Thought maybe they could find the ones who did this."

Every time Ravlon spoke, it was a full-body effort. "With the links broken between the spheres, we can barely communicate to the other casts. I'm...," he choked on more blood, "I'm not sure how bad off the higher angels are."

"How many Dominions rebelled?" Theora asked, caressing Ravlon's bruised cheek.

"Four...five, maybe."

My chest tightened. My shoulders drooped.

Four or five didn't sound like much, but when there were only seven to begin with, the loss was devastating to the cast. More than half of the Heavenly beings governing the lesser angels and commanding the human realm on behalf of the Lord had broken free of any Cosmic restraints holding them on the right side of morality.

If the other two or three didn't get eliminated by their brothers before they broke through the spheres, they still wouldn't be enough to hold the balance in check.

Heaven would certainly begin to deteriorate. God's magnificent but dangerous power would seep through the cracks little by little, burning the Omniverse to ashes.

We needed to find the betrayers and bring them back.

The grim sound of a final breath fell from Ravlon's lips, and Theora released a pained sigh. She murmured a prayer for his soul, knowing there would be no one who'd come to retrieve it and carry it to its resting place in the final destination above.

Even angels had a special world to retire to, but it's doors were only opened by the Reaper...the Soul Bearer.

Rubbing a hand across Theora's back to comfort her, I said my own silent prayer for Ravlon. "We must follow them down," I said, raising off my knees.

Theora looked up at me and shook her head. "I belong here. I was never supposed to leave. Maybe if I hadn't, I could have helped protect the others." A tear fell from her eye.

She quickly averted her gaze back to the angel inside the gates, before wiping her face with the palm of her hand. "Someone needs to stay...in case there are more that come home. I can let them know what's happened." She stood up next to me, straightening her gown while trying to hide the pain and sadness in her expression. "Go. Get Nevaeh. Help her become who she needs to be...for all our sakes."

ARCHARD

HAVEN CAGE

CHAPTER SEVEN

PERILOUS TIMES

"City officials are claiming a sudden increase in all violent crimes. Reports of homicides have sky-rocketed, and our rescue departments are unable to keep up with the calls. They are asking any retired or former police, fire, or medical workers volunteer in assisting with stopping these criminals and helping their victims. Please, if you have any experience in rescue and first-aid, step forward to aid with this growing epidemic of violence.

"Oh, hold on…sorry…I'm getting new information…okay, the numbers for suicides are also on an up-rise. Please, viewers, if you can, step forward to help. Otherwise, hold your families close and abide by the curfews."

I squeezed the remote tighter in my fist and ground my teeth.

This is all my fault.

"On another disheartening note, Jane Dashem is on location, bringing us the most up-to-date story from the fifth monster sighting since Thursday. Jane, what are the residents of Pinehurst saying about these grotesque forms wandering through their quiet neighborhood?"

"Thanks, Barbara. Folks here are boarding up their windows and adding extra locks to their doors. They just don't feel safe anymore. The parents I've spoken with in this sleepy little part of town are pulling their children from school for the next few days, hoping the outbreak of scary creatures roaming their streets will be taken care of by the authorities

47

quickly. The local Police Department is advising everyone use the buddy system when leaving your homes, and keep the curfew, as you've mentioned. If you see any of these creatures lurking near your home, please do not approach them. Some of them have a translucent form like what most would think of as a ghost, others were said to have a broad frame with bits of bone sticking out of their backs. All of them have very gruesome looking faces. Please, beware.

"Unfortunately, between the monsters who've been spotted kidnapping individuals and the humans who are acting uncharacteristically violent, we all need to take every precaution to stay safe."

"Thanks, Jane. We'll hear more about the influx of storms and natural disasters from Greg Underweather after the commercials."

I unfolded my arms and stomped over to the small television sitting on the employee lounge counter. Heaving frustrated breaths, I slammed the damned thing to the floor. Shards of the screen blasted out around my feet, followed by momentary snapping and fizzling from the abrupt disconnection of the electrical circuit.

"Wow, the news was that bad, huh?" an amused voice asked behind me.

Turning to see Nevaeh standing in the doorway, my heart fluttered from a spike of happiness. "Yeah. It's pretty bad out there."

She took three steps into the room then hopped up, sitting on the table where Arianna, her mother, showed Arkin and I visions of how Nev was brought into this world.

Arianna illustrated a past explaining what happened between her, Rhett, and Kenet, how she ended up in purgatory for years, and why poor Nev had to grow up living a life thinking her parents were dead. Everything they did was out of love for her.

It seemed everyone did what they thought was right in order to protect her, but it all ended in failure. Even I had failed. Our love was not enough to keep her soul guarded.

Now, they really were dead. I didn't want to ask her any details about what happened yet. It seemed too soon. She would come to me when she was ready.

I stepped over the mess of broken glass and walked to her, needing to feel her in my arms, to be within a breath's reach. Lifting my hands to her cheek, I looked down into her eyes. I nestled my thighs between her legs. "Did you get enough rest?" I asked, restraining my urge to devour her.

A slight smile pulled at her lips. "I did. Woke up to a spy watching me sleep, though."

I pinched my brows together, bewildered.

Nevaeh rolled her eyes. "Maggie. I felt her staring a hole through my dreams. Figured it was time to get up anyway."

Her hands slid up my hips, slithering under my shirt. The feel of her warm fingers traveling along my stomach caused goosebumps to lift all over my body. I closed my eyes and let her new spicy-sweet scent embed in my senses.

"I'd like to go to church, Archard."

My eyelids popped open.

She was grinning at me. She was completely aware of what she was doing to me. Her hands glided up, brushing over my pecks in the most teasing way. I sucked a strained hiss through my teeth.

"Church, huh?" I bit into my bottom lip as she gently pinched one of my nipples. "What are you planning on doing there? I think it's a little late to worry about attending service to stay in God's good graces, don't you?"

A sheen of gold lettering undulated across her forehead. It was gone in a flash. I stared at her flawless skin, waiting to see it again.

"Well, I thought maybe it would help to say a prayer for my mother and father. You know, as a form of atonement. I hear it's good for the soul to get it all out. I have *a lot* to get out after the past few months."

Nev's gaze lowered to her stilled hands on my chest. The angle took away my view of her electrified amethyst eyes.

Drifting my finger over her jaw, I raised her chin. "If it would help you feel better and move on, I'll take you anywhere you want. Besides, I could use some time in church as well. I have to give thanks for getting you back."

I ducked down, pressing my mouth against her soft lips. Her fingers slipped around my sides and dug into my back. I pulled back, grunting from the sharp bite of her nails.

Nevaeh giggled, seeming to enjoy my discomfort.

"These are perilous times, my brothers and sisters. We need to pray harder than ever before...come together and protect one another," the new priest at St. Julia's counseled.

He was a wiry old man who looked like he could barely hold his rosary, let alone protect anyone.

I glanced over at Nevaeh as she took a seat in the back pew next to me and wondered if Father Varga was still inside her somewhere. Could he see through her eyes? Did he know everything that had happened since his death—since she harvested his soul?

Nevaeh leaned her side against my arm, propping her elbow up on the back of the bench. Her eyes were glued to the priest who'd replaced Father Varga, lit with amusement. I searched her profile, trying to find some indication of the remorse she claimed to have before we arrived, but came up empty.

"Let us stand and say the Apostle's Creed," the priest invited. The rather large congregation stood in unison. Father continued, "I believe in one God—"

A sultry laugh disrupted the prayer, causing the priest's head to jerk toward the sound...the sound that pealed from the woman at my side.

Father shot her a stern look, and Nev cleared her throat to rid the giggles bubbling from her chest.

He prompted his parishioners to restart, "I believe in one God, the Father Almighty—"

Another laugh spurted from Nevaeh's lips. The entire congregation turned in their pews, gawking at her with expressions of disdain and disapproval.

Nevaeh shifted in her seat, her laughter dying. She stood, moving into the center aisle. "Come on, people," she pleaded, "You can't see how that's funny? Look at everything going on around you. Look at the fiends wandering your streets. The folks that used to be your family, friends, and co-workers are either killing themselves or someone else."

I hopped up from the pew, moving to follow her, but hesitated when I realized the effect she was having on these people.

Pausing half-way up the aisle, she rested her hands on her hips then spun in a slow circle, making eye-contact with everyone she could, just as she'd done to the angels in the training room.

Her voice deepened. "You can't possibly *believe* He," Nev pointed to the life-sized crucifix behind the alter at the front of the church, "is still around, listening to your prayers."

Confusion broke out on the worshipers' faces. They were hypnotized by her every move.

"Do you really think He'll be the one to judge you in the end?" Her mouth quirked at one corner. "What if I told you *I* could offer you absolution? That *I* could tell you your judgement right now? All you have to do is open yourself to something bigger than the bullshit this pathetic excuse for a priest is feeding you."

My jaw clamped shut, and my fists curled tight. The shell that softened around my heart when I got Nevaeh back hardened to steel.

This was not *my* Nevaeh.

"I want to know," a shaky voice called out. The crowd of people in the third pew began to flatten against the seat, so a petite woman in her thirties could pass.

Nevaeh's smile widened, her focus zooming in on the parishioner approaching.

"I need to know where I stand with...Him." The woman clutched a pearl rosary to her chest and glanced shyly at the crucifix behind the altar then back at Nevaeh.

Nev dragged her tongue across her teeth. She eyed the woman, assessing her scuffed shoes, the run in her hose, her modest yellow dress, and her gaunt face.

Nevaeh's eyes twinkled. She seemed to enjoy the silent tears streaming down the poor woman's cheeks.

Whatever this woman had done to bring about her internal doubt was weighing her soul down like a cement block in a lake.

"What's your name?" Nev asked.

"Jan," she replied with a sniffle.

"Come here, Jan." Nevaeh opened her arms.

Jan traversed the last few steps between them, nervously fidgeting with the rosary beads in her hand.

Nev wrapped her arms around the slight lady and held on tight. They peered into each other's eyes like two people carrying on a conversation only they could hear.

I hurried down the aisle. The flicker of gold lettering slithering under Nev's left cheekbone caught my eye. It swirled around her jawline, circled her mouth, and climbed the straight ridge of her nose before disappearing between her eyebrows. I slowed momentarily, my fascination with her power overcoming my thoughts.

Opening her mouth, Nevaeh exhaled loudly. A black, wispy tendril floated past her teeth, curling in a ring around Jan's head.

"Don't," I shouted. My words echoed off the towering ceiling but fell on deaf ears. "Stop, Nevaeh."

No one in the congregation moved a muscle to help. They didn't even flinch at the sound of my voice.

I glanced at the priest, who was kneeling in front of the altar, and quickened my pace. Somehow, she had managed to entrance everyone in this damn place.

As a billow of pitch-black substance puffed from Nevaeh's mouth, I snatched her arm, breaking her connection with Jan.

The tendril and cloudy puff retreated through her nose and lips.

Jan gasped, appearing surprised to be standing in the aisle. She frowned, searching her fellow parishioners for an explanation, but they looked just as shocked as she did.

"What do you think you're doing?" I snarled, tugging Nevaeh toward the exit door.

She sputtered and coughed, stumbling to keep up. "I...I don't know."

I looked over my shoulder. She shook her head and massaged her worry-creased forehead roughly.

Pressing my lips together in anger, I shoved the doors open. We stopped on St. Julia's front steps.

I couldn't even appreciate the first rays of sun to break through the constant storm clouds in days.

I let go of Nev's bicep and raked my fingers through my hair, unsure of what to do next.

Her arms wrapped defensively around her middle. She watched a bird peck at the ground below us. She was hiding from me.

"Look at me, dammit," I demanded.

Her gaze slowly lifted, but she didn't speak.

Stepping forward, I studied every twitch, each nuance, of her body language.

Was this the new her?

Or is someone else in there taking over?

"You are not the girl I knew. Who are you?" I whispered. The violet streaks around her black pupils rippled.

A tear rode the crease of her nose, landing on her top lip before her tongue swiped it away. "Archard," she whimpered, "I told you I wasn't the same. I can't help it you're not listening."

Grinding my teeth, I averted my eyes to a passing car. I couldn't bear to look at her. I didn't want to accept that the connection we had before might be damaged by all that had changed. I just wanted the old Nevaeh back. I wanted this version of Nevaeh gone.

Her hands slid up my elbows and along my triceps, pulling me closer. "Please, know that it's me in here." She dipped forward, kissing my forearm tenderly. "It's just going to take some time to get back to a normal routine."

"Nevaeh," I barked, yanking away from her touch, "you are far from normal. What was that shit in there?" I thrust a hand toward the closed church doors. "They couldn't take their eyes off you. You nearly let that demon inside you out. God knows what you would have done to that poor woman had I not stopped you."

She shook her head, denying what I said. "No. No, I'd know if it was escaping." Her brows creased. She looked at the doors, confused.

After a minute of biting my tongue and trying to figure her out with no luck, I decided we couldn't stay there. I stomped down the first two steps at St. Julia's.

"Where are you two going?" Malach called, emerging from the church's west side.

MALACH

CHAPTER EIGHT

INVASION

I skirted the side of the St. Julia's, tugging on a long trench coat. Since spending more time with the Earth-bound angels, I'd taken to following Archard and Arkin's clothing habits.

"Well, are you gonna tell me where you're off to or just stand there watching me with a smug smile on your face?"

My teeth clenched around a sharp inhale as my wings retracted enough to be concealed under the cumbersome garment. That, unfortunately, was another necessary habit I picked up. It was much more painful for me than it was for them though. I had less practice getting accustomed to the discomfort of hiding my wings, and my more pure nature rebelled against the action with a vengeance.

"Oh, I don't know," Archard teased, "I kinda like you being in pain. It helps make up for dealing with your asshole-attitude all the time."

It wasn't a complete lie—I was sure he did like seeing me suffer to some degree—but I knew his jabs were mostly insincere.

We'd come to respect one another while navigating our grim situations. We'd both lost our wards in some fashion and failed miserably as Guardians. We were both trying to make up for it now.

I flipped him my middle finger, unimpressed by his joke, and waited for him and Nevaeh to descend the stairs.

Once the two reached the sidewalk, I could feel the tension spanning their bodies.

Archard cut her a side-glance every so often, his face taunt with pent up emotion. He was like me in that way too—always hiding our true feelings behind our strength.

Neveah's tension was different. Her posture was stiff and guarded as if she was defending herself. She stood slightly behind Archard, her pensive eyes glittering back at me.

When she traversed the portal in Gavyn's apartment and left this realm, Nevaeh was a different animal than the one standing before me now. I could sense her intentions to make things right then. Today, all I could feel was a wall I couldn't breach. There was a chill and disconnection that swirled in the air around her.

She had indeed changed.

I narrowed my eyes, dipping my head toward her in a polite greeting. "Nev. Nice to have you back."

She smiled, some of her chill waning. "It's nice to be back."

"Gavyn?"

Her gaze darted to the back of Archard's head. Archard opened his mouth to answer for her. "This isn't the pla—"

His words were hushed by muffled screams piercing through St. Julia's heavy oak doors.

Archard and I met gazes then bounded up the stairs, bursting through the entrance. Echoes of the wood smacking against the narthex walls paled against the shrill cries begging for help from the cherry pews.

We ran, side by side, toward the noise of splintering wood and horrifying groans.

A spray of blood showered the beige industrial carpet, creating dark spots of tragedy that would never wash out.

I yanked my sword from its sheath and barreled toward the demon gripping a young woman in its thick arms. The monster stabbed a jagged, hooked blade into her chest repeatedly. Its arms raised and lowered in jerky motions, while dry lips pulled back over its yellow, pointed teeth.

The woman's eyes fixed on me, her mouth stuck around a silent scream. With her last harsh breath, the hand she'd used to fend the demon off fell to the ground. A string of rosary beads unwound from her fingers and clattered to granite tiles decorating the base of a small baptismal font.

My gut knotted. I lunged for the Crucio, swinging my sword in a high arc. The torture demon dropped the limp body in its arms like she was nothing more than trash then swerved out of my reach.

In my peripheral, I counted five other Crucios attacking the congregation. Dead human bodies were slumped over the pew backs and piled on the floor. Pools of wet crimson glistened under the church's pendant lanterns.

I ignored the commotion around me and targeted the demon I'd missed, determined not to fail again. It shuddered in a wide circle around me, calculating its odds.

Without warning, I jumped forward, punching its large head with a force so strong, the sound of its short neck snapping resonated against the church's vaulted ceiling.

The demon expelled a screech, but the sound came out gargled through the awkward angle of its neck. Its lofty head hung backward, dangling adjacent to the bony protrusions of its crooked spine, unable to straighten again.

I hoisted my weapon up and leaped into the air, thrusting my blade downward. The pointed tip of my blade pierced its oozing skin and sank into the monster's throat. Satisfaction filled my veins as the sword slid vertically into its chest cavity until my hilt bumped into rotted collarbones.

The demon's jerking quieted. It fell to its knees. I yanked my sword out, appreciating the long, sharp ring made by the metal scraping the demon's vertebrae.

Archard roared behind me, slicing a dagger along another demon's stocky neck.

The delicate inscription of our angelic language gleamed next to the thin edge, guaranteeing the monster would meet its end. They never stood a chance of surviving after a good reaming from our blessed weapons.

"Stop!" Nevaeh yelled over the echoes of demon screeches and human screams.

As I swung my sword over my head, the Crucio in front of me stilled. Its charcoal eyes froze on Nevaeh, waiting for her to give a new order.

From the corner of my eye, I noticed her walk between me and Archard. She held her arms out at her sides, palms and fingers slightly curled up at the ceiling as if holding an invisible ball. With deliberate steps, she approached the alter platform.

A string of mumbled words fell from her mouth. I couldn't understand them, but I knew each syllable was laced with power.

At Gavyn's apartment, when Layla commanded the Aether demons to attack Nevaeh, she spat out something similar. I felt the same uncomfortable prickling sensation ride up my spine then too.

In perfect synchronization, the Crucios left standing held up a gnarled, blackened finger and swiped it downward in the air, ripping a fiery seam in the atmosphere.

Each slit expanded into a yawning portal. They clambered through, the portals accepting them like a mother inviting her children home. After swallowing each putrid being back into her bowels, Hell sealed the veil again.

The only evidence left of the demons' presence were the corpses scattered around St. Julia's, demon and human alike.

Nevaeh's body stiffened. Her head shot back, and her mouth opened wide. Pitch black tendrils swirled out of her, sparking with purple lightning.

Archard stomped past me, his gaze pinned on Nevaeh. I reached out and grabbed his upper arm. He stilled, snapping his head in my direction. Unasked questions lined his face.

"We have to see how far this goes. If this is part of her Reaper gifts, she needs to learn how to use them." I turned back to face Nevaeh, loosening my grip on Archard's bicep.

The dark substance rolling from her body rippled throughout the worshipping area, blotting out every lamp in the building. Night surrounded Nevaeh, Archard, and myself, flooding the aisles. Flashes of amethyst electricity highlighted Nevaeh's body. In the strobing light, she moved to the elderly man hunched over a pew-back to her right.

"Nevaeh, you have to harvest their souls. You are the only one who has the ability now." I shouted over the frenzy of racket coming from her power.

If she heard me, she made no sign of acknowledgment. Her darkness thickened. It was hard to see the zaps of energy through the black cover swarming tight to my skin.

The heaviness I felt from Nevaeh was suddenly overpowered by the pulse I knew only came from Heavenly beings like myself.

My gaze drifted from the lower level of the church to the balcony above the exit door. Beyond the dense tufts of black roiling over my head, I caught the reflective glow of angelic eyes watching us.

"Archard," I yelled, trying to get his attention. I hoped he sensed the intruders as I had.

HAVEN CAGE

ARCHARD

HAVEN CAGE

CHAPTER NINE

A Moment In Time

"Archard," Malach shouted over the booming drone of Nevaeh's beast. I squinted into the inky blanket, but all I could see were flickering beams of electricity. Stepping forward, I followed the muffled words coming from Malach's general direction.

The hairs on my nape stood on end. I stopped, detecting a shift in energy. There was a second power invading the church. It layered on top of Nevaeh's, drenching the atmosphere in a magnitude of supernatural dominance.

I lifted my gaze, skimming over the glimpses of white-robed angels and saints in a scene of Heaven painted on the ceiling. Turning slowly, I surveyed the depiction until sections of the loft became visible through Nevaeh's storm.

Mercury eyes shone through wisps of black clouds — eyes I recognized from my days as one of the Cherubim.

Jacan.

His mouth pulled at the corner, confidence exuding from his grin.

Haunting murmurs sprang to life behind me. I spun toward Nevaeh, squinting through the hurricane of her beast.

She stood stock-still, staring in the shifting streaks of light running through her shadows.

After a few seconds of distraction, she stooped beside one of the humans—a fragile old man with the lines of his face fixed in terror—and leaned down until her lips were brushing his.

Her back bowed around a deep inhale as she called the man's soul to her. She inhaled again. The faint vapors of an extinguished spirit lifted from the deceased, swimming up to fill Nev's mouth. She swallowed the soul as if she'd done it a million times, then rose, approaching the next dead human.

The beastly storm thickened, blocking my view of Nevaeh. I looked back to the loft where Jacan observed Nev's actions with amused interest.

The Dominion stretched his great ghost-white wings out behind him. He leaped over the banister and soared along the rafters.

"Nevaeh!" I bellowed, watching Jacan disappear in her clouds. I sprinted for the front of St. Julia's, but it was like running in a maze with a blind-fold on. Calling Nevaeh again, I navigated the aisles, slamming my kneecaps against several pews along the way.

Hands reached out of a puff of black and grabbed my shoulders. Malach's grimacing face appeared. "Wrong way," he mouthed. His finger shot out to my right. "Over there."

I couldn't tell if it was the sound of a train barreling around me, which seemed to get louder as I neared Nevaeh, or the fear pulsing in my blood that muted his words.

Malach shoved me in the path he'd indicated, falling into step behind me.

I rushed through a dense patch of Nevaeh's beast, landing in a cleared space at the foot of the altar. Nevaeh kneeled on the floor beside a dead woman lying in a pool of her own blood. She worked, harvesting the lady's soul, despite the intruding angel landing behind her.

Malach bumped into me, nudging me forward.

The Dominion's face sharpened into hard, corrupt lines and angles. The white of his wings might have been pure, but his demeanor was littered with bad intentions. I could feel it in the way he looked at me, full of disgust and resentment.

"Move away from him," I urged Nevaeh, but she didn't budge.

Jacan smiled and raised his hand, pointing a golden scepter in my direction. A spark of white light spread from the swirled crystal secured in its tip then shot out toward me.

Gritting my teeth, I lunged for Nevaeh.

I froze the second Jacan's discharge of power hit me.

JACAN

HAVEN CAGE

CHAPTER TEN

Dismantle The Chain

The petite woman bent over a middle-aged female that had fallen at the claws of a demon. The one they called Nevaeh bowed her back and breathed in, drawing out a spirit.

"So...you're the new big bad," I said, bending to examine the dead woman over her shoulder.

Her head jerked up, greeting me with a suspicious gaze and furrowed brow.

With her soul-bearing connection fractured, the tendril of the soul she was eating retreated into the corpse's mouth like a rabbit into its hiding hole.

"What do you mean?" she asked. Her eyes drifted to the edge of the churning black mass blotting out most of the light in our immediate area. She observed the poor excuses for angels held motionless in my time-break.

I tsked. "Come on, Rhett. Don't be coy."

Her head inclined, eyes studying me with approval. She grinned. "Well, well...you are certainly smarter than those two."

I held out my hand to help her up. She slipped her fingers around mine and stood. "I've waited years for you to find your way out of that hole. What took so damn long?"

Rhett crept toward the Earth-bound angels, scrutinizing the mix of fear and fury on their aging faces.

It wasn't very noticeable, but I could tell the effects of this wasting realm on their bodies. Their hair was duller. Their skin was beginning to crease under the pressure of time passing faster here.

Why anyone would want to live like humans, I couldn't fathom. And the stain of betrayal on their wings? I examined how my long feathers swept the floor as I shifted my weight, comparing them to the deep purple of Archard's. Who would give up the Holiness that brightened our very being? All for a wretched human.

My eyes roamed over Rhett's new form, disgust curdling my spit. I gulped down the terrible taste and advanced, anxious for him to hear my proposal.

"What are your plans now that you're out? Surely, you have something in mind."

Rhett looked at me through violet eyes. "I do."

I waited for him to elaborate. He merely put his hands on his slim waist and bit his lower lip, considering me carefully.

"Why should I tell you? Who are you to me?"

I clenched my jaw, holding back a comment that could very well piss him off and ruin our budding partnership. "I'm the angel who broke Heaven's ranks. I'm a Dominion. You should have more respect, Guardian."

His thin brow arched with curiosity, unaffected by my threatening manner.

By the stubborn set of his dainty chin, I could see I'd have to give Rhett some indication I was on his side before he opened to me.

I squeezed my fist tighter around the long handle of my scepter and lowered myself to the requirements of the lesser angel. "We heard she came back from Hell. It was either going to be her fulfilling the prophecy or you. I got fed up waiting to hear who won from the lessers. Figured I'd get the ball rolling either way.

"My true brothers and I spied on this troublesome group, then on you. There was something off about her." I gestured a hand at Rhett's current vessel. "With the way her little friends were watching her like hawks, I deduced that something unsettling had happened while they were in your realm. So, I took a wild guess and got it right."

Moving into Archard's line of vision, I stared into his worried eyes and gripped his throat. I squeezed hard enough he'd feel a bruise when I unleashed him from my will.

"I wasn't about to wait until the next exchange of power to break free of His chains. Especially, when this filth is down here, living his life how he wants with no punishment." Letting go of Archard's neck, I spun to face Rhett. "I'd like to help you. Create an alliance, if you will."

"What makes you think I need help?" He stalked a tight circle around me. His shoulders were relaxed, his energy calm.

He was interested.

"I want to open the veils...converge the platforms. Live as free creatures, unbound by the laws of a single god. We can be our own gods.

"I've taken His ability to control us out of the equation. He wouldn't dare raise His hand to interfere, not with His precious humans at risk of complete annihilation in His presence. He'll wait until the last minute to act, hoping that Nevaeh will save everyone because she is 'the Clavis.' By then, it'll be too late. "

The very idea that God created a half-demon Celata, possessing an ability which allows her to cross our portals like she's walking in the fuckin' park, really chapped my ass. I'm a leader of angels. I don't have anything like that in my little toolbox of mystical goodies.

Placing a friendly hand on Rhett's shoulder, I leaned in close. "I took hostages. I can help you break through the gates of Heaven and, with her gifts, we can dominate all existence. We could dismantle the chain, link by link, then rebuild it how we want." Straightening, I smiled and measured his expression. The twinkle in his eyes told me he was already on board. "So, does that align with your plans?"

He hesitated, then opened his mouth. The hurricane of judgement whirring through the atmosphere retracted into the depths of his new body like smoke in a vacuum. Sucking the last rebellious threads in, he pressed his lips together tightly, swallowed, and offered me a satisfied nod.

ARCHARD

CHAPTER ELEVEN

WHY WOULDN'T YOU WANT TO?

The world stopped on its axis for a single second. All that I was—breath, blood, and molecules—froze. My last thought halted on the idea of getting Nevaeh out of danger.

When the following second ticked by, my flesh and bones unlocked. I stumbled forward, with the sense I'd lost time.

I searched for Nev. Thoughts of her being ripped from my grasp again induced a barrage of unsteady, fear-laden palpations in my chest.

She sat on the top step of a lifted platform. Saint Julia's simple stone altar stood behind her, crystal chalice and wine jars perfectly positioned atop it, untouched by the demons' attack.

Nevaeh's forearms draped over her thighs, and her head hung as she stared at a splatter of blood soaking into the tan carpet.

Jacan was nowhere in sight.

"What happened?" Malach questioned, stepping cautiously toward her.

I crossed my arms, fighting the urge to go to her and wrap her in my love. My girl was in there somewhere, I could feel it, but there was an unpredictable energy slithering under her skin that scared the shit out of me.

"We were in a time-break. What the hell do you think happened?" I piped up, answering for Nevaeh.

Malach glared at me like I was a child who'd spoken out of turn. His focus returned to Nevaeh, and he sat down next to her.

I paced the blood-dyed floor in front of them, awaiting her explanation.

"Did they hurt you?" he asked, pulling her leather jacket aside then lifting her arms to inspect for injuries.

Nev shook her head, her eyes glued to the drying red patch.

Malach probed further. "What did he say?"

"Nothin' really," she whispered.

I jarred to a stop, fisting my fingers tight around my biceps. My eyes grew to the size of a dinner plate. "You can't be serious," I argued. "He had an agenda. A Dominion isn't going to show up here and freeze time just to tell you 'nothing.'"

Her gaze met mine, but she kept her silence.

"What did they want?" I asked, forcing myself to calm.

Malach gripped her arm, pulling her attention from me. "I know you've gotten used to fending for yourself in the last few months, but we are here to help you. You have to help us too, though. What did they want, Nevaeh?"

She looked to the friendly, peace-promising angels on the ceiling. Her shoulders wilted in resignation. "They want me to use my powers and work with them to gain control over the human race." The words crossed her dry lips with indifference.

Malach blew out a loud breath, noting his resolve. "Okay. We can use that, maybe lure them into a trap somehow." He eyed the empty loft where the Dominion spied on us before he descended and incapacitated us with the flick of a wrist.

While the Archangel thought about a plan to thwart the malicious angels, I studied my charge. I took in the planes of her face, noticing how they had changed under the stress of Hell. They were harsher, less of her young softness shone through. Her tense muscles tightened her posture. That glimmer of who I'd loved was dull but lingered just under the surface.

None of this felt right. *She* didn't feel right. I didn't know what to do about it, though. How could I be sure?

If we left her here, assuming she wasn't the good-hearted Nevaeh we hoped she was, we ran the risk of leaving her alone without any protection against the Dominions. What if she *was* who we wanted her to be? What if she held true to her good nature?

If we took her with us, welcoming her into our plans, our lives, she had the potential to destroy all those who fought for peace...especially me. My heart wouldn't survive if her darkness won and she defiled everything we'd done to get her back, everything we'd sacrificed.

"What if I don't want to?" Nev's meek voice asked.

That simple question sucked all the air from my lungs.

What if she didn't want to?

Why wouldn't she want to help? Was it as I suspected...the beast in her won, and we were already too late?

Malach's back went rigid. He shifted on the step, mindfully readjusting the length of his sword along his thigh. Apprehension darkened his green eyes. "Why wouldn't you want to, Nevaeh?"

She shrugged, her attention bouncing between me and Malach. "I...I just don't know if I'm strong enough. My powers are confusing, and I just got home. I don't think I'm strong enough to stand against them. At least, not yet." She frowned, bowing her head again like she was trying to hide her weakness.

I stepped closer, anxious to hold her, but caught myself and settled back into a slow pace.

Malach shook his head, resolute. "We can figure this out. You were born for this, Nevaeh. God has given you more strength than you realize. Fighting is what you were made for."

She popped off the step and pushed past me.

"Where are you going?" I asked.

Nev paused without looking at me. "We're going to need more help if you plan on me taking down a group of rebel angels."

Glancing at Malach, I shrugged, unsure of who she was talking about rallying for our cause.

The Arch rose and followed her out of St. Julia's.

I bit my upper lip and trailed after them, working to silence the siren blaring in my brain.

HAVEN CAGE

CONFESSIONS OF A LOST SOUL

Ah, there you are.

Yes, you. I can feel you, peeking into my mind, watching from your cozy little corner.

Go ahead, disregard the chill brushing your shoulders. Pull your blanket of ignorant bliss a little tighter around you.

Don't, for a second, assume you are untouchable, though. No one is untouchable. We can all fall from grace. Let's face it...everyone has a price.

You just haven't been pushed to find yours yet.

Huh, don't you worry, you'll get your turn to test your limits soon enough.

I know what you're thinking. You think I'm a villain. A devil in disguise. Am I though? Really?

See, I view myself more as a cheated child of God who was forced down a path that led me to be this embodiment of roiling emotions I am today.

If your father forced you to do something, knowing good and well that the outcome might be bad, yet he did it anyway...wouldn't you be a little sore at him?

You would. Don't try to deny it.

I know you better than you think. I've watched you from afar, while you've watched us. I've gotten a taste of who you are at your very base during this little journey we've been on. Felt your emotions. Heard your outrage. I've even noted the chinks in your armor as you've lived this life with us. That's right, I have an idea of what makes you thrive.

And I'm sure you can find some sort of understanding for my part in this. After all, it's only fair. Why should I not be allowed to tell you my side of this adventure?

Let me tell you a story.

Boy is fashioned by the hand of God, breathed to life by the very essence that spins the universe.

Boy is told he is special and given a purpose.

He gratefully fulfills his duty schlepping souls across borders built to keep peace among the supernatural beings, delivering them to their final resting places.

Boy bonds with each soul, finding something special in every single one, even the evil spirits. He commits them to their eternities days on end.

Then, one day, he's told his duty has changed. He is assigned to a human. Forced to guard her.

Guard her, I did.

As she sprang to life, her newly planted roots dug deep into the Earthly plane. They also wrapped around my heart, tying knot after knot along each of my veins. There was no way I'd ever be able to cut the ties that bound us. Or at least, I thought.

Years passed. I remained in her wake, learning from her, protecting her…loving her.

One day, I noticed what seemed to happen overnight; she had become a woman. It was like the sun switched on inside my soul. The roots around my heart tightened, and the blood pumping in my veins heated with a new purpose.

I didn't just guard her anymore, I *lived* for her.

There were moments when I would graze my fingers along her bare shoulder, or nuzzle my nose into her velvety dark hair, and I'd still be too far away from her because she didn't know I was there. She couldn't look back into my eyes when I stood right in front of her, memorizing every royal-blue fleck in her irises.

My body ached to feel her touch me back...to *know* me.

The evening came when I made my decision and shed my anonymity. The beauty of her body illuminated by a blue moon, water gliding over her naked curves like silk, stoked my burning for her to an unbearable level. I couldn't deny our connection any longer.

The moment my lips pressed into hers, tasting her for the first time, feeling her skin react to mine, I knew belonging to her wholly was more important than any punishment I'd receive for breaking an angelic rule.

Next came the visions...visions of words that etched themselves into my mind, blaring at my conscience like a horn until I wrote them down. However, writing them down only made them more of a haunting reality to a future yet to come.

Message after message fell upon my shoulders, screaming in my ears. There was no soothing the relentless anxiety picking at my brain as if it were a wet scab.

While I drowned under the barrage of God's words, my love, the one human I'd devoted my life to, fell for a demon.

Let me ask you something. Have you ever had your heart broken? How about by somebody that was connected to you at the center of all you were? Their life depended on you. Their spirit was so entwined with yours that their afterlife depended on your guidance and care. Have you ever felt a love like that?

Arianna chose a demon over me. She ripped open my chest, severed every artery and vein, and dug out my heart with a spoon before she fed it to Hell.

Then, she had his fucking baby. A child who I was told could bring about the end of everything.

Tell me what I'm supposed to do with that? You, tell me how that made me the villain?

That's okay, I'll accept the role. I have to admit, I made one hell of a mess in my bed. Guess I'm lying in it now, without any reservations.

After I fell from God's glory whole-heartedly — because, let's face it, I sure as shit wasn't going to devote my miserable life to Him after what

He did—I found my home in Hell. Decades of serving another controlling bastard didn't make me happy, though.

I decided, then, I needed to stop dedicating my freedom to other beings. I would get out of the pit of eternal fire and suffering and get my revenge.

God told me that Arianna's daughter was special, that she had the power to change existence. I set my sites on using her power to change the balance for us angels. The only way to get to her was to assume power in Hell, though.

Months of concocting my plans to level the playing fields led me to the perfect moment. However, there were a few long seconds in which my plans hit a speed-bump, derailing my fate like a train plummeting off a cliff. My carefully placed actions to gain freedom and power, in fact, chained me to the underground.

I gutted the Devil with an angelic dagger I'd bribed a Dark Celata to steal. It only cost me a promise to set him free when I received my due authority.

Oh, I got the power to punish sinners and to command demons to do my bidding alright, but I was even more trapped than before.

Who would have thought that the darkness of Hell would cling so tightly to its leader, digging its razored claws into his essence so deep there was no way to escape.

I guess, Hell will always have its Dark Prince…one way or another.

GAVYN

CHAPTER TWELVE

So Far Out Of Whack

It felt like I'd been down here for years already. My blackening heart told me to forget about those I loved; I was just a distant thought in their memories now. My head knew I'd only been in Hell for maybe days, but the strange nature of the place had my senses so far out of whack, I couldn't keep track.

The time here was enough to drive a man mad, even if he was crazy to begin with.

"Have you heard anything, yet?" I asked Dominic for the fifteenth time.

He shook his head, frowning. "They're searching the Dark Celatum, but none of the Aethers have managed to find a stone. They said that Bron stole the one he gave to Layla from the Devil before him. He gave it to her, so she could breach the portal with you and Nevaeh."

"Fuck!" I roared. "There has to be another one around here somewhere."

Dominic shrugged, sinking harder against the wall behind him.

"You can sit in the chair, Dominic." I gestured with my hand, inviting him to take the recliner across from my bed. "You might as well get comfortable...I have a feeling we'll be here for a while."

He glared up at me. "I'm fine here," he responded through thin lips. His arms folded tighter around his knees, pressing them harder into his chest.

I exhaled, frustrated with his refusal to warm up to me.

Stomping over to the wall opposite Dominic, I yanked my blade from the hole-ridden plaster then returned to my original spot. I raised my hand next to my head and flung the knife at the wall again.

This was how I wasted the most recent bit of immeasurable time. We'd decided staying in the skin room with Bron's corpse wasn't exactly appealing. I brought the little shit to the room I'd called home after becoming a Dark Celata until we could figure out a way to escape.

A choppy knock banged at my door. I glanced at Dominic, noting his stiff posture. Holding my hands out to motion he stay calm, I called, "Who is it?" I slunk toward the door, angling my ear in to hear better.

"It's one of them," Dominic whispered, fisting a handful of my pant leg to stop me. "Don't answer it...please." His eyes rounded. He silently begged me to stay sealed up with him in this tiny corner of Hell. He was begging me to keep out the monsters.

Slowly, I turned the knob and cracked the door open.

A Crucio demon bared it's rotting, black teeth and greeted me with a series of recognizable screeches and clicks, saying, "We have souls needing punishment, Master. What will you have us do to them next?"

My gaze shifted around its oozing, decaying shoulder and landed on a woman kneeling naked on the dirty floor. Bruises colored her pale skin like blotches of paint on a canvas. Long, swollen welts crisscrossed over her body like red lace.

Her head lolled around in a lazy circle, trying to see who the demon was communicating with, but it was useless. Puffy eyelids, likely from months of weeping during torture sessions, were all but tacked shut. She sputtered through cracked lips as if praying for mercy, but only a mouthful of blood and drool came forth.

Didn't she know?

There was no mercy down here.

A second Crucio let go of the slouching man it was holding, allowing him to tumble to the ground like a log. He didn't make a sound or flinch when his face planted into the dirt.

Pulling its arm back in a jerky arch, the second torturer stabbed the woman with a two-pronged pitchfork. Rusted points pierced her back and emerged through her front. Blood gleamed at the tips a hair above both of her collarbones.

She gurgled on a pained wheeze as the Crucio spat on her and commanded she not speak unless spoken to.

In that moment, rage unfurled in my gut. I bit down on five words I knew would change me if spoken.

Boil her for disrespecting me.

The withheld command for punishment was acidic, burning a hole in my tongue. It wanted me to wield my new authority in a kingdom I didn't want to rule.

The seductive fingers of darkness crept up my neck, squeezing tight when I crammed the woman's penance down.

What scared me more was how hard I had to fight it.

How long would I be able to deny this entity determined to over-rule any scrap of decency I tried to retain?

Taking a deep breath, I glanced down at Dominic. A surge of strength shot through my body. "Put them in a holding cell for now. I'll deal with them later."

The Crucio in front of me screeched in protest. Its black eyes narrowed. "We cannot give them a moment's peace, Master. They deserve constant castigation," it retorted.

"Are you disrespecting my orders now? Maybe I should have you punished."

The demon ducked his large head. "No, Master, I'm merely reminding you of how things work down here. Helping ease your transition. You are new to this. It is much responsibility for such a...," its top lip pulled up in a grimace, "a man."

"Put them in a cell, and don't touch them until I give you orders, demon. If you disobey, I will have every inch of decaying flesh stripped from your stinking body. Do you understand?"

After a moment of the Crucio weighing the consequence, he barked an order at the other demon. They gathered the tortured souls, dragging them into the dimly lit tunnel.

I closed the door, allowing my hand to linger on the handle as if it would keep it sealed tighter.

"They will be back. They won't wait forever," Dominic whispered.

Resting my forehead on the door, I blew out a breath and closed my eyes. "I know."

It was inevitable, I'd have to either break free of Hell somehow, or give in. Nature would demand the balance, no matter the cost to me. There was no third option for me.

I lifted my head to watch Dominic scuffle to the chair and pull himself up into it. He curled into an awkward, lanky ball against the cushions.

This poor kid had been through the ringer. It wasn't just me stuck down here. I owed him a chance to escape if nothing else, even if I was trapped for all eternity.

"We'll find a stone," I promised. "I'll get you out of here, if it's the last humanly thing I do."

ARCHARD

CHAPTER THIRTEEN

I Pray Your Hope Is Enough

"They plan on meeting at the abandoned fluorite mine at the end of White Oak Boulevard. There is a small waterfall there that empties into the ravine at the bottom. Jacan feels that I'll be able to focus my power better if I have a solid earth base combined with water to conduct it."

The herd of Guardians packed in the meeting room, murmured and bobbed their heads in agreement as Nevaeh spilled the details of what she and Jacan discussed at St. Julia's.

Malach opened the discussion by telling us what destruction the Dominions had caused on their way out of Heaven and how the gates were locked. He informed us about the Soul Transcender being broken and that those who'd died after it cracked were still trapped here.

This was too much for Nevaeh to take on, but there wasn't anyone else. She was the Clavis.

I leaned against the wall in the back of the room, flanked by Arkin and Maggie on one side and Malach on my left. We watched her, analyzing every move...every word. I could detect the same skepticism rolling through their minds as did mine, but none of us wanted to say it.

Keeping her eyes pinned to Nevaeh, Maggie whispered, "Ya know, when I went to your room to check her out, it was like I *knew* she was different, but I couldn't quite put my finger on it. Then she pulled me in. I couldn't help liking her, feeling like she was a true friend." She paused, tipping her head. Her emerald eyes glazed over as if she was refocusing her sight to analyze Nev in a different light. She raised a cocky eyebrow and pursed her lips. "Now? I don't like her all that much."

Arkin nodded. "Yeah. There's something about this entire deal that rubs me the wrong way too. She's just too damn unaffected by everything one second, then trying too hard to seem confused and sad the next."

"She's like a Monet painting...it's pretty to look at, drawing you to look closer and make you think you like it, but when you get too close, it's just a big mess of colors that don't make sense. It's not right, I tell ya." Arkin threw up his hands then slid down to the floor. He frowned, listening to the rest of her speech while fiddling with a frayed thread in the seam of his jeans.

"So, I'll approach them inside the ravine, and y'all surround us along the upper rim." Nevaeh gave the attentive angels a wide grin. "That should give us the advantage we need." Her eyes shot to Malach, and she nudged her chin toward him. "Meanwhile, the Arch will teach me how to use these new powers of mine."

Malach pushed off the wall, standing tall with his head high. He tucked his thumbs in his leather belt, letting his hands rest there while scanning the crowd for protesters.

Most of our group had accepted him as one of us, though there were a few that still enjoyed pissing him off just because they could. I had to admit, I was one of those few. We were just jealous because he could still cross the portal to Heaven, where the rest of us couldn't.

It was a punch to the gut each time he left us here in our chosen misery to glimpse the majesty that was once our rightful home.

Nevaeh continued, "When the time comes, I'll do my best to trap them in my storm, so Malach can collect the Dominions to mend the ranks."

A gruff voice piped up from the far corner of the room. "If the gates are locked, how do you plan on planting their asses where they belong, Malach?"

Malach's head dropped, and he inhaled. When he looked back at Gareth, his gaze filled with belief and determination. "Nevaeh is the

Clavis. It's my hope that she can open the gates. If she can open portals, maybe she'll be the one who can release the lock."

Gareth searched the other angels' faces. A low chuckle erupted from his mouth then built into a robust fit of laughter. He doubled over, slapping his thigh. Moments passed while he struggled to gain control over his outburst. Swiping tears from his eyes, Gareth settled himself to a few random guffaws and shook his head. He stood from his seat, saying, "Well now, brother, I pray your *'hope'* is enough...because if it isn't, we are all up shit's creek without a paddle—humans and angels alike."

The doubtful angel took a step to leave, but Nevaeh moved in, blocking him from the door.

"Do you wanna see what I'm capable of?" she purred, staring up into his eyes.

Gareth's tense face relaxed, his body swaying an almost undetectable amount. He didn't answer her, only returned her stare.

Maggie gasped beside me. Shoving off the wall we leaned against, she inched forward with her gaze pinned to Nev.

I took my hands from my pockets and moved to her side. "What? What do you see?" I asked, studying Nevaeh and Gareth.

She shook her head, gulping hard. "I...I'm not sure. Their bubbles have changed. He was a deep midnight blue; now, he's a dull gray-blue. And she...," Maggie blinked, glancing down at the floor, then back up at Nev. "She was a muddled blend of colors, but no lavender."

"So...now, there's lavender?" I could feel the wrinkle of tension forming on my forehead, trying to figure out what Maggie was implying.

Her slim fingers curled around the crucifix on her neck. The chipped black paint on her short nails made her hand look harsh as she smoothed her fingertips over the ridges of Jesus in delicate strokes.

A slow smile formed on the pixie's raisin-hued lips. "I only caught a smidge of it in your room before. It was just a shimmer of light. Couldn't even see her color. Now that she's using her powers, though, it glows like a fuckin' lighthouse. I remember detecting it when I saw your casts at the old house Bron snatched her from…when she tried to take your soul," she said, her voice quieting when she mentioned the last part.

My eyes shot from Maggie to Nev. "She's using her powers?"

"Yeah, she's doing some kinda hoo-doo shit." Maggie's features twisted in concentration. "I don't know…hypnosis, I guess."

Watching Nev drill holes in Gareth's eye-sockets with her gaze, I noticed the sheen of gold ripple across her cheekbone before disappearing into her jaw.

I nodded with understanding. "It makes a little more sense. When she uses her powers, the book writes on her skin…or, rather, the writing appears on her skin. The same thing happened at St. Julia's. The congregation hung on her every word, like she had them in a trance. It must be one of her new gifts from the book."

"Or, it could be someone else," Malach said, his posture bone-straight. He looked over his shoulder at me. "I know I was the one who's been insisting Nev is actually Nev, but…," he dipped his head toward Maggie, "she can see to the core of a being's soul."

I held up two fingers in a half-wave, dismissing his explanation. "When we were in Hell…before we came back…I killed Rhett's Devil form." Combing my hands through my hair, I ignored the shame pounding its way into my bricked-up heart. "I killed him, and she ate his soul."

The trio eyeballed me for a moment, digesting the new tidbit of information I'd given them.

"You couldn't have known what would happen, Archard," Malach comforted. "That makes things coincide so much more, though. I think we can agree we've all thought about it." His gaze shuffled between each of us. "What if *that's* not Nev?" he asked, pointing an accusatory finger at Nevaeh. "What if she is Rhett? Perhaps, he's syphoning her power, and it pulls her to the surface." He scrubbed his hand over his jaw, then met my eyes. "What if she's trapped inside her own body with the other souls?"

Clenching my teeth, I rolled the obvious possibility around in my head.

Malach added, "We...angels...put humans in trances all the time, without intending to. It's part of our nature. Rhett's ability to do that likely magnified as the Devil. On top of that, they share soul-bearing capabilities. He could easily do what we expect of her in that position.

"She commanded the demons at the church too. That was something Layla did. Nevaeh harvested her soul too. Rhett could draw on Layla as well."

I blew out an exasperated breath, feeling like I'd been kicked in the gut. We all knew it. We all second-guessed who she really was. We just chose to believe she was Nevaeh rather than facing the truth.

Maggie rested her hand on my forearm and gently squeezed. "She's still in there, Archie."

In the background, I heard Nevaeh command Gareth to sit back down, and the sharp scrape of a chair sliding across the floor indicated that he'd obeyed. She asked the crowd if there were any other angels who wanted to test her new gifts. No one spoke up.

A small whimper of disappointment escaped Maggie as she removed her hand from my arm and resumed worrying her crucifix. "He's got her buried again. The lavender light is dim, but it's still in there."

Arkin stood and wrapped his arm around Maggie's shoulders. "So, we just need him to use her powers more."

Our heads whipped toward Arkin.

"We get him to use them more...maybe, it'll pull her out enough to evict the bastard somehow. Right?" Arkin bit his bottom lip and focused his attention at the front of the room where Nevaeh beamed back at us.

Her sweet lips curled into a smile.

I wanted to puke. The thought of Rhett keeping her hostage in her own body, of him thinking he had us all fooled, made me sick.

Malach leaned forward to see around me and address Arkin. "I don't think it works like that. She won't be able to just evict him. She'll have to expel him. Deliver him, somehow. Like the other souls still inside her. With the Soul Transcender broken, I'm not sure how she can do that."

"This is all his fault. Mother-fucker doesn't deserve a deliverance to Heaven," I grated, keeping my expression as relaxed as possible, so I wouldn't tip Rhett off that we were onto him.

The Archangel nodded. "Regardless, that's not up to us to decide. She'll have to make that judgement."

Maggie turned toward Malach. "So, what do we do to help her escape?"

Malach squeezed his eyes shut and pinched the bridge of his nose. "I'm not sure."

"We'll make her use her powers…it's our only choice right now," I said.

"And, if that just heightens his skill…deepens his hold on her?" Malach asked.

I straightened my slouch of defeat, mustering up whatever conviction I could. "We'll deal with it."

MALACH

CHAPTER FOURTEEN

Now, Sing.

"You really think this is the best place to be practicing? They could be watching...the Dominions, I mean." Nevaeh tucked her hands in her jacket pockets and scanned the uneven ledges looming over us.

The sun was nearly set behind the rocky cliff. The evening air promised just enough chill to combat the thick, balmy climate sticking to us as we ventured into a night of learning what Rhett was capable of.

I led her to the point where the cliff's rough facade began to smooth. It disappeared behind a steady rush of the Durant River spilling over the lip of solid stone two stories above. The water's continuous drone and rainbow spray, created by its descent to the pool below, made the hidden treasures of this area seem even more mystical.

Nodding, I examined the crystal facets embedded in the wall. Catching the last rays of sun, the gems left behind reflected prismatic hues of purple, blues, and green amid the dull stone encasing them. "Yes, this is a great place to start. We'll be better equipped to fend them off if we know the battlefield. And," I reached out, tracing a particularly large facet of blue peeking out of a ridge, "these stones will help you focus your energy. The fluorite the miners left untouched will clear negative energies. It'll let you reconnect with who you really are...you know, deep down in your soul." I gave Rhett a pointed look, noting how uncomfortable he seemed.

Good, he needed to be uncomfortable.

"They really couldn't have picked a better spot." Perching my hands on my hips, I spun in a slow circle, admiring the layout of the area. We were surrounded by the tall crags on all sides except for the entryway. The workers had cleared an access along one side of the river's path out of the valley.

"Malach is right," Maggie said. She wandered closer, her gaze trailing over the rocks then landing on Nevaeh. "I can see it already." A knowing grin tugged at her lips.

Nevaeh's face scrunched up, confused. "See what?"

Maggie traipsed around Nevaeh, eying the space between them, detecting something the rest of us couldn't. "How your aura is reacting to the vibrations here. You're usually scrambled with colors," she raised her hands and shook them, mimicking the frenzy that was Nev's energy, "but, here, they are starting to calm, to unwind from each other."

Nevaeh slit her eyes, following Maggie's circle around her. "I'm not sure what you're talking about, but I hope it all works in our favor. It would be devastating if the Dominions won, right?" She tore her gaze away from Maggie and looked at Archard, who stood next to me.

He drank her in, the wheels of his troubled mind spinning at a hundred miles an hour. Archard nodded. "Yeah, devastating," he deadpanned.

I clapped my hands together and started toward her. "Well, shall we get started?"

Nevaeh cleared her throat nervously, glancing up at the ridges one last time. "Sure."

Maggie and Archard settled on a flat-topped boulder beside the water and waited for us to begin.

"I want you to clear your mind, Nevaeh. Close your eyes. Picture the power of the book swimming through your body."

Her cautious frame relaxed when she closed her eyelids. The sharpness of her expression softened. That was the Nev we all remembered. The cocky, sweetness that wrapped around her and touched all our hearts trickled out, if only in the shadows of her demeanor.

"We know you can call your storm out, and you seem to have a handle on harvesting souls. We need to concentrate on opening portals."

Her chin tipped up. She smiled, her eyes still closed. "Yes, let's."

Nevaeh held her left hand out to the side and snapped. Balling her fingers into a tight fist, she wound her hand in a large oval. Purple light streaked behind her movement, manifesting a bubbling, blistering hole in the atmosphere. The small window of Earth we saw inside the oval burned to ash and blew away on the breeze, revealing a chaotic view of Hell.

My angelic instincts kicked in the second I saw the hazy winds and burnt-orange mountains of the Devil's wasteland. I inhaled, breathing in the sulfuric scent of everything I fought against.

"Good," I said through gritted teeth, "you can close it now."

Nevaeh dragged her tongue across her teeth lazily, her grin widening. Rhett was toying with us.

He hesitated for a moment, then exhaled loudly like a disappointed child. Snapping his fingers again, he traced Nevaeh's fist in the opposite direction around the oval and sealed the portal shut.

I released the tension in my muscles and unclenched my hands from around my sword hilt.

In my periphery, Maggie whispered something to Archard then resumed watching us.

"Now, open one to Heaven," I ordered.

Archard jumped off the boulder, taking two strides toward us. "What? No," he protested.

I held out my hand, motioning for him to stay where he was.

Maggie hopped down, hurrying to his side. She whispered something in his ear again.

Archard's shoulders slouched, and his jaw tightened. Once he accepted what she'd said, he shook his head then returned to the rock.

Studying Nevaeh's now expressionless face, I stepped closer. Thin, glowing-gold letters fanned over her right temple before disappearing under her eyebrow.

"How do I do that?" Rhett asked, eager to learn what he didn't know yet.

My gut screamed that he already knew—being a former angel—but maybe he just couldn't figure out how to do it in Nevaeh's body...with her powers.

I was walking on dangerous territory. In one hand, I was teaching the enemy to do precisely what we didn't want him to do. On the other hand, I hoped it would pull Nev out enough to gain use of her faculties and fight Rhett. We needed her to take back what was hers. The world needed it. There were so many souls waiting to be laid to rest, and none of them would have that chance if Rhett's plans took hold.

"For us, Heavenly beings, it's a matter of using our angelic call. Try singing. See what happens."

Nevaeh chortled. "You want me to sing?"

"It's worth a shot." I looked at Maggie and Archard leaning against the rock, ready to play the defense if anything unexpected happened. "Just focus that hum of energy running through your limbs. Try to concentrate in your throat, around your vocal cords."

A line of letters rippled from under her shirt collar and swirled around her neck, the glow intensifying as she concentrated harder.

"Now. Sing."

ARCHARD

CHAPTER FIFTEEN

Evict That Motherfucker

I held my breath, waiting for the first note to leave Nevaeh's mouth.

Malach's theory made sense; Angels could open the veil to Heaven with strategically belted songs, so I imagined he hoped Nev could do the same. I knew it would be harder than he thought, though. She was no angel, nor did she have any angelic vocal cords to manipulate the notes just right.

My ears perked at the first soft hum resonating from her throat.

"That's it. Like that, but louder. Open your jaw wider to give the sound some freedom," Malach instructed calmly.

Nevaeh's eyes popped open. Glaring at him, she huffed out a breath. "There's gotta be a better way."

Setting into a measured pace around her, Malach cocked an eyebrow and said, "If you have another idea, please share it."

She glowered at him, a hollow forming in her cheek from her biting on it.

The Arch flipped back his tan, ankle-length coat, securing it behind the shiny weapon fastened at his hip. He rested his hand on the sword's pommel, eyeing Nev as he came to a stop at her left.

"Let's try again, shall we?"

Nevaeh rolled her eyes, pushed her shoulders back, then inhaled a deep breath. She closed her eyelids and relaxed her jaw, letting it fall open in a deep yawn. A velvety sound drifted from her mouth, increasing in volume as the air from her lungs blew through her voice-box.

Maggie stiffened at my side, shoving off the rock. I followed her line of sight to Nev's upturned hand.

The empty space above her fingertips wavered like heat vapors on hot asphalt. Nev flexed her hand around the translucent waves, squeezing the air in her palm as if molding the molecules of power gathering there.

When the last of her breath released, the air stilled.

"Again," Malach bellowed. "Do it again."

Nevaeh inhaled another breath. She sang harder and louder this time. The glowing gold letters floating under her skin like leaves in wayward water intensified. The waving patch of air resumed at her fingers, stretching farther from her hand.

She inhaled again quickly then belted out another long note before the blurring air normalized. The pitch of her song fluctuated, becoming higher. Her distinct sound took on a new articulation, splitting into two separate voices layered in a strange, robust call to the heavens.

The undulating space extending up from her palm twisted, wobbling from side to side in a drunken tornado.

"It's working," Maggie muttered, her wide eyes stuck on Nevaeh. "It's working, Malach," she yelled. "Don't stop her."

Nevaeh's back bowed, thrusting her chest up toward the sky. She stopped singing. Heavy breaths rushed in and out of her trembling body. Her face screwed as if she was enduring some kind of torture on the inside.

"Again," Malach barked. He clasped his hand around her wrist and yanked it toward the stars. "Sing, Nevaeh," he rasped. "Come on, girl. You're almost out. I can feel you in there."

She grimaced and shook her head, growling at Malach.

I lunged forward, needing to hold her in my arms. "Maggie? What's going on in there?" I shouted, leaving her frozen frame in my wake.

"She's breaking out. Her cast...it's unraveling," Maggie answered urgently.

My gaze fell on the fading blur churning above her head. I clenched my fists and sprinted to Nevaeh. Wrapping my arms around her chest, I tugged her trembling body toward the river, snatching her from Malach's hand.

"What are you doing, Archard?" he yelled. "I had it under control."

Nevaeh thrashed in my arms, but I tightened my grip to keep her against me. "Water. The water will help ground her," I spat. Stumbling over the river rock lining the banks, I lost my balance and tumbled with Nev into the flowing river.

I lifted her head above the surface. She coughed and sputtered, clearing the water from her nose and mouth.

"Come on, baby. We can do this," I pleaded. "Don't leave yet." I pulled her deeper into the river. "Maggie," I called, "she still with me?"

Maggie nodded excitedly. "Yeah, but he's digging his dirty claws back in. You better work fast, Archie."

I swam with her until the water swirled around our chests then spun her to face me. Narrowing my eyes, I searched her glossy irises. Her lips quivered. Her body shook. I couldn't tell if it was from the cool river or from the turmoil happening in her soul.

Ringing my fingers around her wrists like manacles, I raised them between us. She stared blankly at me, but the flickers of light buried deep in her gaze let me know she was attainable.

"Nevaeh, baby, you have to sing. Just a little more," I begged.

Her brows pinched together. Her nostrils flared, and she sealed her lips shut tight.

My heart sank when a deep giggle flitted from her chest.

I was losing her already.

No. She's right there, I thought, sensing a slight tug in the thread that bound us together at our centers.

"Dammit, Nev." I shook her wrists roughly, trying to grab her attention. "Sing for me. Evict that motherfucker."

When I didn't get a reaction, I crashed my lips into hers. I kissed her until my mouth hurt, until my lungs were depleted of oxygen, until the sizzle of energy that always pulled us to each other zapped from her to me.

She jerked free, gasping like my actions had jump-started her back to life. The violet electric flickering around her irises shifted. Nevaeh's jaw slackened. After a slow draw of breath, she forced out the sweet sound I longed for.

One voice. One soul shining through. And it was one I recognized with absolute certainty.

Blurry waves sprang forth, curling around Nev's flexed fingers. I spread her hands apart, allowing the portal to spin and grow as she sang.

Nevaeh maintained eye-contact with me while lifting her hands higher into the air.

I smiled, my grip releasing enough to slide down her arms and skim over her sides.

She was back. I could feel her soul reaching out, yearning for that constant embrace it always hunted from mine. I would gladly give it to her. I would embed every piece of me into her very life if it meant keeping her here.

The wind picked up, causing tiny goosebumps to raise on her skin. I adored the way her flesh warmed under my touch.

I reveled in the way her ribs stretched around each deep breath, the sound of her heart pounding in my keen ears, the sweet smell of...*her*...just her.

The spinning blur above us widened. Droplets of water trickled up from the river. They gathered around the rim of the portal Nevaeh was opening, dampening the air she manipulated.

Light poured out from the center, casting a radiant indigo haze on Nev's soft curves and lean muscles. More of the river reached to meet the roiling portal. It churned and spread into the silvery funnel indicative of Heaven's veil.

As she continued to sing, a quarter-sized opening formed in the middle of the portal.

For the first time in decades, I saw a glimpse of home. Tears filled my eyes. My heart warmed. My mind wandered to memories of carrying my God's throne on my shoulders, being engulfed in His glory and love.

I missed who I used to be more than I thought. Yet, when my gaze skimmed down from Nev's hands, taking in her strong body and beautiful face, the love I felt looking at her was paramount to the memories I'd had moments before.

Nevaeh's expression tensed. Her eye twitched, and her cheek ticked. The energy it took to maintain the veil's opening was wearing her down.

"That's enough, Nev."

She ground her teeth and squeezed her eyes shut, not hearing my words.

I put my hands on her cheeks. "Stop. You can stop."

Her eyes opened, that familiar violet electricity stirring while she registered my words. "I can't. He'll come back," she cried.

"I'll help you keep him at bay." I rested my forehead on hers, wishing I could crawl into her skin and keep her protected from the force fighting for her body. "Stop, now," I said softly, before kissing her.

In the distance, I heard Malach say, "That'll do, girl." His tone was light-hearted and pleased.

"Will they be okay here?" Maggie asked, concerned. "I mean, she's still with us at the moment, but what if Rhett comes back?"

"Archard will fight for her. It's what he was made to do. Let's just hope this is the end of Rhett."

Their footsteps trailed off, leaving me and Nevaeh to fend for her life.

HAVEN CAGE

NEVAEH

HAVEN CAGE

CHAPTER SIXTEEN

HE WAS MY KEEPER

I can't believe it.

My mind was quiet. My body was mine.

My galloping heart was his.

The vibrations of the rocks and the hum of the river surged through me, heightening the power burning in my blood. As we devoured each other's mouths, power drew from me, like threads tugging on my fingertips. It would almost tickle if it wasn't so damn demanding.

Archard pulled away, panting from our kiss. He reached his arms up and laced his fingers between mine, urging them down around his neck.

The moment he broke my stance, the portal sealed, the bright indigo light dissipated, and the river water fell on us in a light rain.

"My God, I've missed you. I've missed the way you taste, the way you feel. It's been too long, love," Archard breathed, studying my eyes.

I hiccupped a sob, so thankful he found me. Here, in *his* arms, I felt safe. I felt like...*me*.

When the last of my gift dwindled away, we were doused in the mysterious splendor of the yellow moon. Stars flickered in the vast sky, shining down on us approvingly.

I burrowed into his warmth, rubbing my hands through his hair, fisting his wet locks gently. He smiled and tightened his arms around me. His fingers dug into my back, pulling me as close to him as possible.

Our mouths joined again. Our tongues tangled, lapping at one another like the greedy flames of need burning in our cores. Our breaths mingled, blending the honey and lavender aromas that were solely us.

His hands scoured my torso until he found bare skin at my waist. Archard shoved my floating shirt up out of the water and over my head. He tossed it to the bank where it landed in a soppy mess.

His gaze drank in my expression. I was certain the fear of being swept under Rhett's raging tide and the desire to entrust everything to Archard showed clearly on my face.

I wasn't the only one battling my emotions. Doubt and hope warred in his eyes as transparently as the water engulfing us.

He skimmed his palms over my shoulder blades and around my sides, stopping when his hands molded over the curves of my breasts. My breath hitched. The hunger escalating in his eyes met the insatiable need building in my core.

The chill creeping into my body from the river disappeared under the blaze of his touch. My nipples beaded under his fingertips, coaxing a strained growl from his throat.

I lolled my head back, wanting to give my body over to Archard, but scared that, if I did, Rhett would assume control. I struggled to maintain the moment of clarity and dominance I had, wondering how long it would last.

Rhett was still inside me. I could feel his grimy essence polluting my being.

"Hey," Archard murmured, gearing my attention back to him and his roaming hands, "be with me?"

I gasped from the sensation of his hands brushing along my hips, tracing the edge of my jeans. I swallowed hard and exhaled a resounding, "Yes."

Archard's fingers popped my button loose then lowered the zipper. He pushed the water-logged denim down my legs, and I kicked the rest of the way out. He tossed them overhead to land on my shirt.

The river sloshed around his chest as he took off his own clothes and threw them in the pile with mine.

A shiver of excitement rode up my spine.

Memories of my gravitational pull to Archard when I first saw him, learning what pain he'd endured when he gave up his Holiness to protect me, and the severance of our connection when he showed me my fate flashed through my mind. We would always be a part of each other. He'd sacrificed so much for me.

He was my keeper. I was his to keep.

Archard placed tender kisses along my forehead, nose, and chin, moving lower at an unhurried pace. I dipped my head back, letting him suck the droplets of water from my throat and kiss my neck.

He wrapped his strong arms around my torso and waded me backwards. Moments later, the rush of the waterfall showered down my back. He pressed me into an eroded rock protruding slightly through the fall. Though the water was cool, the fire burning between us was plenty to keep me from noticing.

His fingers worked to unclasp my bra. He slowly lowered the straps off my shoulders. Tugging the plain, black cotton down my arms, he let it drift away on the bobbing waves.

The watery surface licked at my breasts and splashed over my shoulders. My angel dropped his gaze to the wetness shining on my chest, consuming every visible inch of my flesh.

Archard hoisted me up, guiding my legs around his waist.

He stared at me with an overwhelming brazen passion. I gulped back my fear of Rhett's looming control, fear of an uncertain future, and fear of what would become of us. Closing my eyes, I held onto his shoulders for leverage and lowered myself onto him.

My world stopped spinning. The river's steady rocking seemed to halt. My nerve endings imploded, shooting zaps of pleasure throughout every tiny crevice of my body.

Having Archard inside me, filling my depths, claiming me, might be the closest to Heaven I ever got.

Hooking his arms beneath mine, he curled his fingers over my shoulders and inched me down more, sinking deeper inside me.

I moaned, resting my forehead on his, fully conquered by pleasure.

Completely seated in my core, he stilled. "Look at me, Nevaeh. I need to see your eyes."

Opening my dazed eyelids a fraction, I met his gaze and grinned.

He released a breath of relief, finding what he sought.

"It's still me," I assured him. "I'm with you." Locking my ankles behind him, I eased up then settled back down onto him.

Archard groaned with my motion. His worried expression morphed into a look of repressed need. He set into a rhythm of his own, taking control of our movements. He splayed his hands along my back, shielding me from the rough surface of the rock as he moved in and out of me.

Tilting my head back, I reveled in the massaging pound of the waterfall soaking the crown of my hair. I basked in the love radiating from our joining, moaning when he plunged into my depths time after time.

He buried his face between my breasts, planting ravenous kisses over my breastbone before moving to the side and capturing one of my nipples between his lips.

I arched into him, welcoming the tingles he spurred along my nerves.

We made ripples in the water and love in the night until the tension became too much.

Our bodies exploded like two supernovas blasting in space.

Coming down from the dizzying whir of passion, I relaxed my legs, letting them float in the river as Archard slipped from my heat.

"Now what?" I asked, keeping my arms wrapped around his neck.

He caressed my jaw with his finger, wiping away the droplets of water there. Sweeping me out from under the waterfall, he trudged us toward the bank. "We should go back to the warehouse for now, I suppose."

Helping me stand on my jellied legs, he walked us out of the river. Archard bent over to collect our clothes. I stopped in my tracks, seeing him fully naked for the first time.

Sure, I'd felt him, but seeing him was an entirely new experience. Faint shimmering lines in the shapes of feathers glowed on his skin in the moonlight, marking where his wings hid. Hard muscles and deeply cut valleys tensed, shifted enticingly with his movements. He was breathtaking.

He wrung out our damp shirts and pants. When he turned to hand me mine, he paused, raking his eyes over my bare frame as I had done his. He licked his lips and smirked.

"You're so beautiful, Nev," he complimented, holding out my pants. "Instead of going home, I'd be happy keeping you right here, naked and wrapped in *me*, for a few days."

I offered him a weak smile, appreciating his sweet words. I was too afraid of the unpredictable future to enjoy his playfulness, though.

Taking my jeans from his hand, I dropped my gaze and focused on getting dressed.

"I know we can't stay for days, but what if we stayed just a little longer? Do we have to go back this second?"

Already dressed, Archard stepped closer and dragged my shirt over my head, helping me put it on. He brushed strands of wet hair from my face. Holding my cheeks in his hands, he looked into my eyes. "I'll do anything you want, Nev. Anything to make you feel whole again. I would've stayed in Hell just to be by your side."

"I just…," I exhaled a frustrated breath, "what if we leave here, and Rhett comes back? What if it's this place that keeps him away?" I wiggled loose from his hands. "I can't go back to living in his shadow, Archard. We have to find a way to get him out of me."

Though I was facing away from him, I knew he was right behind me. The constant friction that passed between us when we were close told me he'd countered my steps away from him, maintaining our nearness.

His arms encircled me, and his hot breath seared my neck as he spoke. "It's not this place, Nev. These rocks…that river…they just help you magnify what is already swarming inside you. It's your faith, your gifts. The strength you find in trusting them prevent him from taking over. You just need to remember that if he starts to weasel his way back...at least, until we can find a way to exorcise him from your body."

Archard moved around me and clasped his hand with mine. "Come on. We'll stay a while longer."

I trailed him to a large rock flattened by years of machines scraping it away in search of Fluorite. He laid on the hard surface and waited for me to join him.

I lowered, cuddling in tight to his side. My head fit snug in the crook of his arm. I closed my eyes, hoping his love would be enough to anchor me to the forefront of my being.

He smoothed my hair with his other hand over and over until I fell asleep.

DOMINIC

CHAPTER SEVENTEEN

Like Screams In The Grand Canyon

The voices. Someone, please, stop the voices.

I can't keep doing this for much longer. They'll eventually make me completely insane. I'll be nothing more than a bucket of mush demons use as a telephone.

"Dominic. Are you listening?" Gavyn hissed. His face twisted with the rage and anger snaking inside him.

I'm always listening. Doesn't he know that? Whether I want to or not. Someone is always talking to me. I can't get them to go away. And this place...it just amplifies them. They echo against my skull like screams in the Grand Canyon. I can barely hear my own thoughts anymore.

"Dominic. Did you ask them? Can the Devil survive a portal?"

I banged my head back against the wall, hoping to hush some of the rambling demons in my brain. "Why do you want to know?" I wasn't sure I wanted to give him information that might unleash another monster into the human realm.

"If I can survive a portal, maybe I can reach Nevaeh on the top-side."

"And how could you possibly think that is a good idea?" Threading my fingers through my hair, I pulled, ready to yank the strands out by the roots if there was a chance it would get the demons to silence.

Gavyn stomped to the door of his small room and kicked it, the sharp ping ringing through his quarters. He yelled, slamming his fists into the metal. It wasn't a very smart thing to do, considering the slab was as thick and sturdy as a jail-cell door.

In the last few days, or what felt like days, he'd flip-flopped between moods where he was relatively calm and episodes of fury that could surpass the darkest, most hateful creatures by miles.

I watched the war wage inside him while I battled my own war. We were two soldiers in nearly insurmountable crusades.

During his more docile phases, I saw a man that had nothing but honorable intentions; a man that I could have learned to like, had he not murdered my sister. Witnessing his two faces showed me that, perhaps, it was not his true self I was mad at. How could I blame him, when he might not have been the real Gavyn at the time he shot Layla?

I still couldn't dismiss that fact that there was a growing darkness in him now, though. And this evil was likely way more damaging than Gavyn's original bad side.

He marched through the room, throwing the few things he hadn't already broken and punching the dirt walls. "I can't stay here for another fucking minute, Dom. I need to get out of here," he growled. "I need to breathe. Otherwise, I'm going to sentence one of those poor saps the Crucios insist on bringing here to an eternity far worse than you can imagine." He paused in the center of the room and glanced around, a shred of forced calm washing over him.

I narrowed my eyes, debating if I should help him or not. He was right. His mood-swings were worsening. If he didn't get out of Hell soon, it would consume the last of his humanity.

Then I would be trapped in here too.

My shoulders slouched. I dropped my head, dreading the realization of my possible fate in Hell for the umpteenth time.

Closing my eyes, I crawled into my mind. The Aether demons' distracting whispers increased to a concert-level decibel. I squeezed my eyelids tighter and tried to organize the chaos. Weeding through the Aethers that were just talking to be heard and the demons that might offer an answer, I concentrated on Gavyn's question.

Can your Master cross portals?

The hairs on my neck stood on end when their attention zoned in on me. It was like being in the center of a Lion's den with a cow strapped around my neck.

I held my breath, waiting for one of them to step forward and respond.

He can, but he'll never be free of us. He belongs to ussss, they answered in my mind. *He is like you, pet. Never escape.*

A shudder skittered up my back. I knew it was true. St. Julia's was the only place I had found solace, but they were still there, under the surface, scratching at my psyche.

"They said yes, but you'll still belong to Hell. What that means exactly, I'm not sure," I grunted through the discomfort of their invisible claws latching onto me as I retracted from them, distancing my mind as much as I could.

Once I had a grip on my physical reality, their jabbering quieted back down to a disturbing choir of whispers.

"Great. You comin'?" Gavyn bolted for the door.

"Wait," I jumped up from my spot on the floor. "You can't seriously think it'll be that easy. You're just gonna zip out of a portal and be human again?"

His hand stilled on the knob. He spun to face me, his eyes glossing over. "I *am* human, Dominic." Gavyn frowned. "At least, for a little longer."

A tinge of guilt tugged at my heart. "Well...how do you plan on getting a portal open?" I asked quietly.

He grinned. "I figured I could command one of those Animus assholes to clear a path for me." Turning the knob, he opened the barrier that had kept us segregated from the rest of Hell since Nevaeh left with the angel. "We just gotta chase one of them fuckers down." He crossed the threshold, searching the endless tunnel for a monster he could use.

My feet didn't move.

Gavyn looked over his shoulder. A worry-line formed on his forehead. "Come on," he urged, motioning his hand for me to follow.

I shook my head and combed my fingers through my hair.

"It'll be okay. I won't let anything happen to ya, Dom."

I appreciated his confidence and protectiveness, but he couldn't guarantee that. He knew it, and I knew it. Aside from that, there was a bigger problem keeping me from joining him.

"I can't go through the portal without Layla's stone, or without Nevaeh to carry me through."

GAVYN

CHAPTER EIGHTEEN
WE HAVE A DEBT TO SETTLE

My chest constricted. I couldn't leave Dominic here by himself. "How do you know?" I stared at him, trying to work it out in my mind. "If I can breach it, you should be able to piggy-back with me."

He wrapped his arms around his chest, like he was bound in a straight-jacket, and winced. "They told me I wouldn't make it through with you. You haven't accepted your position, so you don't have the power to take me with you."

I huffed out a breath. "Fuuuck!" I shouted, digging the heels of my hands into my eyes. "Can't anything go our way?"

Dropping my hands, I rushed at Dominic. "I don't know what to do. Tell me what to do, Dom." I shook him, hoping it would rattle a happy solution from the voices in his head.

He didn't answer, he only frowned and peered down at his dusty shoes.

I fell to my knees and hung my head, holding onto his forearms. There was only one chance for us to get out of here, but I felt I needed to beg his permission to do it. My attempts might not be worth the risk in the end, but I had to try. This place would turn me into the worst kind of monster if I didn't.

Dominic raised one of his hands, pulling free of my grasp. He placed his palm on the back of my head. "Go."

A tear dripped from my eye and splattered on the floor. We started out on a bad foot, and I would never expect him to forgive me for what I did to Layla, but I liked him too much to leave him here and not think twice about it.

In the small amount of time we'd spent together here, we'd bonded. Enduring Hell can make you best friends with your biggest enemy.

"I know you have to go. The evil will eat you alive if you don't leave."

I lifted my head, staring up into his blood-shot eyes. He kept calm on the surface, but I could see the terror crystalizing in his mind.

"I'll come back for you. I promise. I'll find Nevaeh, and she'll help me spring you free."

He pressed his lips together, holding back the sobs lurking under his composure. Nodding, he tugged his other arm loose from my hand and retreated into the room. Dominic sat on my bed. He glanced around the room warily. "I'll be here waiting for you."

I stood, swiping away another regret-filled tear. "Stay in this room, Dom. Don't open this door for anyone, or anything." Placing my hand on the knob, I began closing the heavy steel door shut. "Not anything, you understand?"

With a nod, he whispered, "Don't forget about me, Gavyn."

"Never." I shut him in—away from the monsters of Hell.

It felt like my skin was glued to the damn door. What was left of my conscience demanded I open the metal slab and sit my ass down right next to him.

I jerked my hand away, shaking my head, arguing with myself in silence. I was taking the necessary action to get us *both* home…right?

Settling on my final decision, I sprinted down the torch-lit corridor to my right. I repeated my promise to Dominic over and over, silently, to keep my eye on the ball.

After two miles or so of running, one left turn and two rights, I broke into a sweat. My heavy breathing and thumping heart were all I could hear, aside from the tortured screams filtering through cell doors lining the walls. Not one demon in sight.

They'd been hounding me since I resurrected; now, I couldn't find one fuckin' lackey.

I skid to a stop, doubling over to catch my breath. Heaving the foul air in and out of my lungs, it dawned on me that I was the new master of Hell.

What if I just commanded one to appear?

The moment the thought sparked in my mind, screeches sounded not more than forty feet away.

"I'll be damned. It actually worked."

Suddenly, my chest felt like it might crumple. A phantom pressure had reached between my ribs, wrapped filthy talons around my heart, and squeezed until I nearly passed out.

The familiar fury haunting me on and off for days returned. Ideas of revenge and domination crept into my heart, muddying my plans to leave Hell and find Nev so I could get Dominic out.

I clutched my chest and slid forward. Sticking close to the wall, I inched farther along the tunnel. As I came around a slight bend in the path, I spotted what I was looking for.

The putrid Animus hunched over, peering back at me with vacant charcoal eyes. Its jaw worked mercilessly behind that seamless flap of skin they called mouths.

I approached it carefully, assessing its body language. The thing let out a piercing screech, followed by a pained grunt, then dropped to the ground on all fours.

Master, it greeted in a disembodied voice which resonated through my head like music.

"Open a portal to the Human realm," I groaned, sucking in gasps of oxygen between the pulsing squeezes around my heart.

The Animus rose, held out its spindly fingers, and pressed against the stony wall. A surface that was hard and unmoving, stretched around the demon's hand with the elasticity of bubblegum. The Animus leaned its lanky, burnt body into the wall. It sank into the perimeter of Hell until the barrier ripped. Clawing at the tear, it opened the portal wider, then stumbled into the space between realms.

I straightened, staring through to the freedom I dreamt about for days...no...months. I'd wanted this since Layla trapped me down here under the false pretense of helping Nevaeh. Since she trapped me in my own weakness. Another agonizing squeeze of my heart reminded me I was still captive.

As I stepped forward, the Animus screeched.

Stop, it warned.

I stilled. "Why?"

Its raspy voice echoed in my head. *Cannot pass. You must embrace power. Never make it.*

I growled. "For fuck's sake."

All I wanted to do was return to my home...to be human again...the man I was before. I could smell the warm bread and sweet ice cream served at my café. The sounds of my regulars laughing and the football game playing in the back teased me. I could feel the softness of my bed and Nevaeh laying in my arms. I could taste her kisses on my lips, envision her smiling at me as she toweled her hair dry before work.

I wanted that normal. And I would do anything for it. If I could just get to her, if I could just set my eyes on her, she'd fix everything. She could fix *me*. I just needed to find Nevaeh.

Inhaling deeply, I let the phantom dig into my soul. I crouched down, leaning against the wall for support, as the crippling pain invaded my body.

Poison blacker than night funneled through my veins. A power unlike any I'd felt before engulfed my senses and seeped into my pores.

Where to? the Animus rasped.

Floating on the high of supremacy, I stood up and filled my lungs with ease. The pain subsided.

A throaty chuckle bubbled up from my diaphragm. "Archard," I directed. "Take me to Archard. We have a debt to settle."

ARCHARD

HAVEN CAGE

CHAPTER NINETEEN

MY HEART SANK

The patter of rain hitting my face jolted me awake. I pushed myself up, lazily looking around the mine. The first rays of dawn were shining on the rocky cliffs caging me in, bringing to life the pastel blue and purple Fluorite peeking out from under layers of dirt. The water glistened through the middle of the mine, calling to mind thoughts of what Nev and I did the night before. I smiled.

For a moment, I had peace. For a moment, I had a chance at love and happiness. For a moment, I had Nevaeh.

My heart sank when I realized she wasn't tucked in my arms. She wasn't wandering the mine, or bathing in the river.

I reached out my senses to find her. A blaring emptiness punched me in the chest, not the glorious warmth that met me when she was near.

She was gone.

I rolled off my side, thudding my back against the cold rock beneath me. Glaring up at the cloudy sky, I felt the wall building around my heart once again, brick by brick. I'd never make it without her unless I hardened my emotions.

Deep in my soul, I knew Rhett had taken her over.

We were back at square one.

After ten minutes of letting the downpour pelt the pain from my body, I shoved to my feet. Tightening my fists and gritting my teeth, I welcomed the tearing sensation accompanying the release of my wings.

A roar broke free from my lips when the thick, white and plum feathers burst from my arms, chest, and back. They repositioned to a more comfortable place between my shoulder blades, solidifying from their tar-like form into soft plumes and gold protective plates.

I inhaled a cleansing breath, relieved of the constant burden of being stuffed in my own body while they were hidden.

I sprinted along the Durant River, adjusting to the weight of my appendages, then leaped into the air. Pumping my wings furiously, I steered toward the factory.

I had to let the others know Rhett had repossessed Nevaeh.

CHAPTER TWENTY

New Game-Plan

Jacan's head whipped around. He held out his scepter, ready to attack, when he heard me coming.

My wet shoes shuffled across the mausoleum's cement floor. Rain steadily dripped from my clothes and pattered against the ground, making my entrance quite noisy.

A sly grin pulled at his mouth. "Well, well, well. Seems we've had a change of plans?"

I slicked Nevaeh's long, wet hair out of my face and glared at him, flinging the water from my hand. "Yes."

During our tryst in St. Julia's, he informed me where I could find him. The graveyard behind the church struck me as odd, but, apparently, it was a wise choice since nobody thought to look for them there.

Scoping out the large underground room I'd descended into from the church's yard, I found four other Dominions lazing about the area. They were all dressed in human street clothes, not the crisp, royal-blue garbs they usually wore. Their eyes roved over me with curiosity.

Huddled in the far corner of the vault, there were two beings bound. The first was an angel with a Principality's crown shimmering faintly beneath his forehead.

My mouth dropped open when I recognized the second figure.

"It's been a long time, Jacan, but is that an...Ophanim?"

I squinted at the creature, allowing my vision to blur ever so slightly. Ghostly outlines of two thick bands of light circled the Ophanim's human-like body. The bands worked in synchronized precision, spinning around the horizontal axis while in constant rotation around the vertical axis. They were the Heavenly Wheels of God.

This was a creature most angels never stood in the presence of, let alone captured. They were stationed in the first realm of Heaven, guarding God, which made them nearly unreachable from the lower levels.

"Indeed, it is, my friend. It's *his* Ophanim."

My gaze flicked up to Jacan. "His?"

He smirked, leaving his perch on the corner of a tomb in the center of the room. Strolling toward the hostages, he answered, "Archard's. We thought it'd be good incentive if things went south. You know, if he doesn't give up on...," he eyed my figure from toe to head and lifted an eyebrow, "her."

Staring back at the Ophanim in awe, I nodded, understanding his theory. "Their spirits were tethered when Archard was a Cherubim. They carried the throne of God together before he became a Guardian."

It made sense. There was not another being that would have such an impact on Archard as this one. I wasn't even sure Nevaeh could hold a flame to this angel.

I examined the Ophanim closer. It didn't have a speck of hair anywhere. A red silk robe barely clung to it shoulders, doing little to cover patches of skin marred by days-old bruises. Spots of a darker crimson stained the garment, indicating cuts I couldn't see beneath the thin fabric.

Scanning back up to the Ophanim's face, I studied twenty or so smaller eyes, in varying hues of brown, blue, and green, blinking back at me. They all shifted independently, keeping track of anything in their surroundings that might be a threat.

Though it was an odd-looking angel, it might have very well been the most beautiful thing I'd ever seen. Of course, it could've been the amped up Grace radiating from it too.

The being opened its pretty heart-shaped lips and spoke in the sweetest voice. "Traitor. You are all traitors," it said calmly. "You think the Father didn't know? You think you won't pay? You should have changed your ways when you had the chance." It blinked its many eyelids.

The Dominion with cinnamon hair stomped toward the Ophanim. He angled his scepter, pointing the glowing orb at the bound creature.

A cry of protest burst from the Principality roped-up next to the Ophanim. "Don't. Please don't hurt her anymore."

The Dominion sneered at the hostages, and a zap of power arced out of the orb.

The Ophanim convulsed from the surge of energy shooting into her body.

Shielding my eyes from the bright, blue light, I peeked around my hand and watched the bands of Holiness encircling her body go hay-wire.

"That should be enough, Calev," Jacan advised.

Calev snatched his scepter back, ending the attack on the Ophanim. She wilted to the side, all of her eyes closing. The Principality leaned in, catching her against his shoulder. He whispered prayers in her ear as silent tears slipped down his face.

"So," Jacan said in a chipper tone, "why are you here, Rhett?"

I tore my gaze away from the hostage angels and joined the Dominions around a map of rocks and sticks laying on the tomb's lid.

"She escaped," I admitted, inspecting the make-shift plot of the mine. Anger flared in my gut, remembering how the Guardians used Nev's power to override my control on her.

Glancing up from under my brow, I continued. "Everything was fine...until they took me to the mine. They must've figured me out. When we got there, the Archangel showed me how to open the Heaven portal with her energy."

Jacan jumped in before I could say more. "I don't see where that is a problem. You know how to use her now, right?"

Eager motherfucker.

143

I bit back a string of curses and answered, "Yes, I know how to do it inside this vessel. But, something about the vibrations of the rocks and the amplification of water allowed her to take the reins."

They pondered what I said.

"How do we know you aren't her?" Calev asked. "How do we know you aren't trying to trap us this very instance?"

I let out a dry chuckle.

Somehow, I'd managed to claw my way back out while Nevaeh was sleeping in Archard's arms and stuff her whimpering soul into the deepest, darkest corner I could find.

"You don't," I answered. "But what choice do you have outside of believing me?"

Jacan raked his gaze over me and crossed his arms, leaning into the tomb for a beat. "It's him," he verified to the others, satisfied with whatever evidence he saw of my true personality.

"Do you have a handle on her? Will you still be able to go through with this?"

Glancing back at the hostages, I assessed my grasp on Nev's body.

Sure, I still felt her in here, along with those other blubbering fools, but I used to be quite a powerful angel. The Almighty chose me to write the Clavis Prophecy, dammit. Besides that, I was the original Soul Bearer. It's in my nature to eat souls, cast judgement, and open the veils. I just needed a little guidance on how to do it with Nevaeh's body. Malach helped me with that.

Next time, I intend on syphoning all the strength I can from Nevaeh, and possibly Layla if I need the extra umph. That dirty girl still had a lot to offer after death.

I nodded. "Yes. I have no doubt we can pull this off, but we need to catch them by surprise."

"And how do you propose we do that?"

I slid my hand along the top of the tomb, scraping the sticks and rocks aside. "Do you know the abandoned factory on Williamson?"

CONFESSIONS OF A LOST SOUL

I wasn't always a bitch, ya know.

Things happened. Things I couldn't control. I did the best I could to cope, but apparently it wasn't enough.

I'm not exactly sure where I went wrong, but I suppose that doesn't matter anymore.

I'm dead.

Guess I got the shitty genes in the family. With a father so evil he shoots the mother of his children then commits suicide because he's too much of a fuckin' coward to face us, I was bound to end up damaged, right?

Dominic was too strong, too faithful, to let that disaster break him.

I tried, I really did. All I wanted was to keep him safe, and, in my mind, that meant having power that could trump these...*gifts*...of ours.

Come on, let's be real. They aren't gifts, they're fuckin' curses.

What kinda god gives two kids the abilities to interact with and control demons? I bet we were some hilarious experiment to him. He's probably sitting up there on his throne, laughing his ass off.

Well, I hope not because I'm gonna need him. We all are.

At first, I thought, *Hey, what's a little mission for the Devil if it'll keep Dom safe?* Then the missions piled up.

I got greedy. I thirsted for the rewards he promised — money to take care of Dominic, a gemstone that granted me power to travel between worlds, authority over some of the Dark Celatum, and love. I could give my baby brother everything his heart desired. I could've done the same for Gavyn too, if he would've only let me.

Looking back now, I see how I let the Devil manipulate me. I mean, come on, he's pretty damn convincing. I'm not the only one who let him make a doormat out of 'em.

Yeah, the problem with telling myself it wasn't my fault is that I deluded myself. It was totally my fault. I had choices. They may have been terrible options, but I had free will. I *chose* to hurt those around me. I *chose* to drag them into my misery and make their lives harder because I didn't want to be the only one suffering.

Life was just too much without my mother. It was too gruesome with the memory of what my father did to her...to us. I couldn't take care of Dominic on my own.

I should've done like my dear ol' dad did. One bullet to the brain would have fixed it all, my suffering, my pain, the pain I cause others, and Dom could have continued his life with Father Varga.

Wait—huh, I guess I did get a bullet to the brain. Didn't help a damn thing, either.

My brother is in Hell, Nevaeh is locked in here with me, Gavyn is dead, and the Dark Master got exactly what he wanted.

I lost everything, everyone dear to me, as a teenager because of tragedy. Then, as an adult, I pushed anybody willing to give me a chance away with my conniving ways.

Well, it's time I take responsibility. Time I step up and remember who I really am, or at least who I want to be.

Sure, it might be too late for me, and, if we make it through this, Nev might throw my sorry ass back in Hell for all eternity, but I will go down knowing I tried to atone for some of my sins.

The Dark Master wants to steal my curse to hurt more people?

Asshole better think twice.

I'll fight tooth and nail to keep it from him.

With all that I am, I vow to stop him from using me anymore. I vow to help Nevaeh anyway that I can.

And I vow to give my soul over to the Light.
Lord, help us all.

ARCHARD

CHAPTER TWENTY-ONE

GUTTED AGAIN

I burst through the doors of our factory and marched down the main hallway, yelling for everyone within ear-shot to gather in the training room.

Heads poked out of doorways, expressions of confusion and annoyance on my brothers' faces.

"Get in the damn training room," I demanded.

They followed behind me, murmuring about what got my feathers ruffled.

The mass of Guardians, and a few Archangels, crowded in around me. I tamped down my feelings of defeat and doubt. I couldn't let them see how close I was to snapping. We had to stay strong for Nev.

"Arkin," I called, stretching my neck to search for him.

"Yo," Arkin answered, skirting the angels to take his place at my side.

"Malach and Maggie?" I asked, glancing back through the jumble of muscle in front of me.

"They're on their way. Had to check on a demon outbreak downtown." He took a swig of the amber liquid sloshing in the mug he was holding. The faint smell of whiskey wafted to my nose. He hated when Maggie went out to address demon occurrences without him. His worried eyes met mine. "It's getting worse, Archard."

I nodded, biting my top lip. "Did they inform you all about what happened at the mine?"

"Yeah, before they left."

Blowing out a loud, contrite breath, I looked each one of my brothers in the eyes and decided not to wait any longer. "It's about to get a lot worse," I warned. Gripping Arkin's shoulder and squeezing gently, I commiserated in his fear.

"Angels, I have some bad news. We had her. For a fleeting damn moment, we had Nevaeh back with us."

Arkin leaned back against the weapons table, slumping under the weight of the same disappointment I felt. His gaze dropped to the floor while the others grumbled their frustrations. A couple of angels left the semi-circle to punch a wall and throw a chair.

"We'll never stop them from opening the veils," Niven voiced.

I stepped forward, searching for a strand of redemption that might pull them back in and give them hope. "She's still in there. We saw with our own eyes."

I glanced over my shoulder at Arkin who was retreating into himself, weathering the storm of fury, defeat, and grief inside. A storm similar to mine, which I refused to acknowledge just yet.

Returning my attention to the group, I said, "We need to find the faith we've lost, my brothers. Hunker down and figure out a way to save her." I said the words, but I understood how they felt better than anyone. I was trying to convince myself as much as them.

"How many times, Archard? How many times will we hold out hope and pray that she saves us...saves the humans...just to be gutted again in the end?" Niven asked, shaking his head at my relentless attempts.

"As many as it takes," I shouted. More bricks stacked around my heart, hiding the fragile organ from the grief creeping in.

My thoughts of distress and loss was interrupted. The cavernous room echoed with the sound of the door banging against the wall. We all turned to look at the entrance.

Nevaeh stood in the doorway, smirking as her eyes roamed over our surprised faces.

Each angel's body tensed and shifted into a defensive stance, creating a barrier of muscle and wings between me and Nevaeh.

I shoved through my brothers and approached Nevaeh hesitantly. My slow steps resonated off the cement floor, adding to the harsh thumping of blood in my ears. I reached my senses out to connect with some remnant of Nev but came up empty-handed.

Rhett had her now.

She was buried deep this time.

"You look a little out of sorts, Archard," Rhett chortled, eyeing the snarl of disgust on my face. "You don't want me here anymore?" The beautiful lips I longed to kiss pushed out into a pout.

"No, Rhett," I gritted, "I never wanted you here. You don't deserve to breathe the oxygen in this realm."

He tsked, sauntering closer to me, wrapped in the soft curves and gentle slopes I dreamed of holding every second of the day.

He let out a humorless laugh. His expression hardened. "I don't think you have any right to cast judgment." Rhett circled me in a wide breadth. "You know, it's rather exhausting playing Nev. You guys are nothing but a bunch of whimpering babies. You're not fit to wear the wings on your back," he sneered.

"Look who's judging now."

"Ah, you forget," he moved closer, stretching Nev's small form up on tip-toes so his mouth hovered at my ear, "I *am* the original judge."

I closed my eyes and forced myself to ignore the lavender scent wafting to me from her hair.

This is not Nevaeh, I assured my body.

"Maybe so, but you gave up that station long ago. Nevaeh is the Soul Bearer now. She is the only one who has the authority to cast God's judgment."

"Mm," he hummed in agreement, "but I'm the soul that controls Nev. She'll never have possession of this body, or her reaper powers, again." He pressed her breasts into my arms teasingly.

I flinched, the sudden clatter of glass shattering filling my ears. My brothers murmured behind me as I raised my eyes to the large windows lining the top of the training room. Five Dominions swarmed through the large opening like wasps on a mission.

They landed in a strategic form with Jacan heading the bunch, and the others flanking him, slightly turned to watch for ambush from the sides and rear.

Each one had their scepters drawn, glowing with Holy power the traitors stole from the Heavens when they left.

My heart jumped into my throat. One of the Dominions man-handled a figure with eyes studding her face.

"Vanna," I exhaled.

She was my past, the second half of my soul before Nevaeh.

I glanced at Arkin. The look of befuddlement on his face mimicked how I felt. How could they have reached her, let alone extract her from Heaven?

"That's right, Archard. You wanna play dirty with your fucking rocks and water tricks? I have tricks of my own." Rhett's nostrils flared with pent-up ire. "Which will it be, Guardian? The Ophanim? Or Nev? You can't save both."

Before I had a chance to answer, Rhett opened his mouth, releasing Nev's beast into the atmosphere. Her lightning cracked and whipped the air, blotting out the fluorescent lights buzzing above.

Three Dominions rushed toward the other Guardians, screaming war cries.

My brothers scrambled to grab weapons from the walls and table. They were strong fighters, and we had the numbers. My stomach still knotted, though. The Dominions were warrior angels from a higher sphere. They had infinitely more power than what our small rank of rebels had.

Arkin drew his ax, engraved with the authority of our Lord, and began swinging at the intruders.

Sizzling sounds resonated in my ears. I spun to see Rhett's hand splayed out at his side, sparking a Hell portal to life. The air singed and burned away, opening the mouth of Hell. It slowly grew bigger and bigger, abolishing the human realm inch by inch.

Jacan and the remaining Dominion hurried to Rhett's side, smirks plastered on their faces. Jacan's sidekick dragged my Ophanim and another angel toward the portal.

"It's time for this non-sense to end, Archard," Rhett shouted over Nev's whirling clouds. "You'll never beat us. It's fate. We were always meant to bring the worlds together."

I called forth the last bit of Holiness I had streaming in my blood. Flames flourished, engulfing my right hand. My fingers melted together, forming a razor-sharp blade. A sharp pain sprung to life as my mouth widened and my teeth elongated into fangs. Shifting into my lion, I released a roar that rumbled against my ribs and the cinderblock walls.

If I could just disable them somehow, knock them all unconscious until I could figure out what to do with Nev, it might buy us some time. I knew, though, if it came down to it, I'd have to kill her. I couldn't allow them to destroy the human realm just to spare the one I loved.

I flexed both sets of my wings and lunged toward Rhett. From the corner of my eye, I saw Jacan raise his scepter in my direction. I braced myself, knowing he'd probably freeze me before I reached Rhett, but I hoped someone would stop him first.

"Uh, uh," someone warned, "if anyone's gonna take him down, it's gonna be me."

I pounced on Rhett, just as a blast of fire hit Jacan. With Rhett against the floor beneath my weight, I looked back. The lead Dominion lay on the floor, motionless.

Gavyn crept into my line of sight.

"Miss me?" he asked, grinning from ear to ear.

MALACH

CHAPTER TWENTY-TWO

JUST A LITTLE LONGER, MY SON

Maggie and I roam the halls of the factory, eager to tell the other angels how much worse the demon attacks were getting among the humans.

Maggie's Light Celata friend, Ginger, had dealt with days of Aether demons haunting her, following her around and chipping away at her strength. Her attempts to dislodge them from her life were pointless. Ginger had called Maggie when she finally reached her wit's end, begging for help. I accompanied Maggie and a few of the other local Celatum to aid in banishing the Aethers.

"I just don't understand how they managed to latch onto her in the first place," Maggie said, contemplating the Aethers' change in nature. "They usually lose their grip on the victim once the person wills them gone. Ginger said she'd tried everything from demanding they leave to white-magic spells. Nothing worked." Maggie shook her head, working through Ginger's predicament in her head.

"I don't know," I responded, veering into the hall on our left. "If free-will won't deter them anymore, though, we're going to have a lot more of these incidents on our hands. Possibly more than we can handle. Hopefully, Nev will be able to hel —"

The thunder of squall winds and men battling cut me off. My eyes darted from Maggie to the door banging closed then swinging open at the end of the corridor. Beyond the cinderblock frame, streaks of angelic power flew across the atmosphere like shooting stars. Angels lunged at one another, shouting their intentions to defend or defeat. Flickers of glowing blue, purple, and green lights reached into the hall, creating a show of warring energies.

A large body with blood-tinged wings soared across the doorway. Maggie gasped. Her eyes bugged, and her hands reached up to cover her gaping mouth.

"Stay here," I commanded, racing toward the training room.

I drew my sword and entered the fight-zone, taking a quick sweep of the situation. Arkin was holding his own to my far right, fighting a Dominion with his ax. The Dominion's scepter lay on the ground, shoved under the weapon table, well out of the traitor's reach. Two of the other ill-willed angels slashed their scepters in the air, firing short flares of power at the Guardians surrounding them.

Sizzling buzzed in my ear like a mosquito, forcing me to turn. My heart skipped a beat the moment my gaze fell upon the hole eating the atmosphere faster than a fire ravaging a dry forest.

Striding against the gales Nev had unleashed with her beast, I pushed toward her and Archard. Better assessing the players in this battle, I dug my feet into the ground two yards from them.

Archard's jaws stretched wide over long teeth dripping with saliva, the sheen of his skin taking on a tawny suede texture. His hair blew wild in the wind as he glared down at Nevaeh, gripping one massive paw hand around her throat. He pulled back his elbow, brandishing his other razor-sharp hand amid the fiery vortex swirling around it.

I slanted my head to the side, focusing on the familiar figure standing behind Archard.

It was Gavyn. My ward. A deluge of remorse flooded me. The boy I'd failed was now a man running so deep with demons his soul emitted the stench of evil.

His slick hair, longer than the last time I'd seen him, dripped sweat onto his pale, thinned face. His dark, green eyes glinted with the promise of revenge.

A strange tether, purplish-red and thick like coagulated blood, encircled his neck and draped over his shoulder. My eyes followed the length of it until the Devil's chain disappeared into the Hell portal.

Gavyn's hand fisted the greasy tether and yanked, snatching another foot of slack from the bowels of Hell. He stepped forward, crooking his neck against the collar, a grimace of discomfort and rage on his face. He reached out, curling his fingers around the ridge of Archard's wings.

As I watched Archard rear back in pain, a small voice rode on the storm, echoing in my ear, but I was too engulfed by emotion and confusion to pay it any attention.

I would rather Gavyn have died like they'd said than him fall to the perils of being the Devil. There he was, though, the binds of the underworld claiming him as its prince. So much power, yet still a slave to the energy of wickedness. An unfortunate weight on the balancing scale of good and evil.

Snarling like an alpha cat provoked into a competition of authority, Archard released Nevaeh and flipped around to meet Gavyn's challenge. He slung his head back, violently shaking it from side to side.

The lion fell away, and Archard's ox came forward. Horns grew from his skull, curving down toward his cheekbones. Archard's mouth elongated into a blunt, nostril-flaring snout. He stomped on the ground with his hoofed feet and thrust his wings behind him for more power. He lunged for Gavyn.

Gavyn braced for the impact, laughing with excitement. The two brawled ruthlessly while the world was going to shit around them.

I glanced at the Hell portal, which now nearly took up half of the large room. A small herd of Crucio demons crossed into our realm, jittering toward the Guardians.

My gaze landed on Jacan. He rolled onto his side and pushed himself up, then stumbled toward Nevaeh. Craning his neck to the Dominion behind him, he yelled orders I couldn't make out through the noise. The lackey Dominion jerked the two beings in his hands, forcing them into motion.

I groaned in pure disgust when I realized they had taken an Ophanim and a Principality.

Nevaeh curled up, gathering her wits, and scanned the room. A sly smile split her face. Her twinkling purple eyes locked on mine.

Suddenly, the voice echoing in my ear became louder and clearer. "She's not Nevaeh," it cried.

A faint grunt of pain piqued my attention, waking me up from the slow-motion reality I'd gotten stuck in. I looked to my right.

Maggie and Arkin fought side by side, disabling the demons and Dominions closest to them. She glanced at me while jabbing an angelic lance into a Crucio. "She's not Nevaeh, Malach," she shouted again.

I gripped my sword tighter, flexing my wings to lift me up. I needed to get above the situation, view the big picture.

My first instinct was to get Nevaeh out of here, but Rhett had her, and he'd already opened the portal. We'd need him to close it to do any good. Otherwise, demons would continue to enter the Human realm by the hordes.

Next, I considered joining the fight, but the Guardians where holding their own.

Then, there was Archard and Gavyn. I had to accept there was no helping Gavyn, and Archard had enough power to keep him at bay for now.

Something in me insisted I was needed elsewhere. I just couldn't figure out where exactly.

My body flushed with the warmth of Heaven, a heat that illuminated my soul with the light of God. I stopped circling above the chaos and hovered with my face pointed to the sky. I relaxed, opening my senses from within, and reached for my creator.

In my mind, He whispered, *wait. Just wait a little longer, my son.*

The warmth dissipated in the blink of an eye. Behind it, came the feeling of loss that always accompanied the gravity of His absence.

The skin on my left leg prickled. I looked down to find the crackling edges of Hell inching closer to me. I swooped away before its evil fingers could sting me but doubled back when I heard Nevaeh's song carry through the large room.

Rhett held his hand above his head, inhaling a deep breath and releasing another haunting note in Nevaeh's voice. Air untouched by the Hell portal undulated and blurred around him. He sang more of the melody needed to breach Heaven's veil with steady determination and smooth vocals.

For a moment, I doubted he'd be able to recreate the power it took last time at the mine. He didn't have the Fluorite or the river to draw power from.

My doubts were dismissed when the blurring waves of this realm swirled into a cyclone of silvery moisture pooling from air molecules and energy syphoning from the Heavens.

Though the fierce need to stop him boiled in my blood, I waited. I prayed that Rhett's stubborn use of Nevaeh's gifts would return her to us.

The mercury whirlpool coiled above everyone's head like a reverse drain, the center gaping wider and wider with each spin.

Gritting my teeth and holding my position, I spied on Jacan.

"Now, Rhett!" he yelled over the heavy storms and sparring mutiny. Jacan grabbed the Ophanim from the trailing Dominion then grabbed the back of Rhett's jacket.

Great, glimmering wings spread out around them. Jacan peered up at me, sneering, as Rhett pressed against the traitor's body and looped his arms around Jacan's waist.

Nevaeh's beast gathered in around the group, a magnet to its master. Surrounded by the dense, light-absorbing shroud, Rhett nodded at Jacan before winking at me.

Jacan launched them all into Heaven, leaving the portals open to eat each other and the world caught in the middle.

HAVEN CAGE

FATHER VARGA

CONFESSIONS OF A LOST SOUL

Faith.

It's a fluid thing.

Most of us go through life having at least a speck of it, but don't think it's enough to keep us in the Good Graces.

When I was a boy, helping as a farmhand in Tura, I'd trudge across acres of land to get to the church before dawn.

It was *my* church, the Catholic Church of Hungary.

My roots were steadfast in my beliefs, and I always knew I'd grow up to be a part of the clergy in some way. Years later, after my anya passed from pneumonia and my apa died at the hands of a drunk farm-owner, I devoted my life to faith. It was all I had left.

I've never regretted a day of it.

From my faith sprang years of delivering lost children to the hands of God. It's been the most gratifying life a poor Hungarian boy like me could've imagined. Dominic is a prime example of this. He's been my prize on this Earthly plane. He let me know my intentions did not go unnoticed. Even in a life, where blood- family is forfeited to be a leader of the church, I found a son in Dominic. I can only hope, one day, far in the future, we'll see each other once again.

Though I have faith I'll attain the happiness I dream of, my time has not yet come. There's still work to be done.

I currently find my soul trapped in limbo, at the will of a being who's lost his faith and rooted himself deep within a young woman who holds the weight of the world on her shoulders.

Her faith was fluid, too, like ocean tides pushing and pulling against an unstable shore.

If I've learned anything in my years, it's that most lost souls, with even the smallest speck of credence in the Lord, only need a nudge in the right direction to find their way back to the path again — no matter how many times they stray.

I can feel this child's light in here with me. It's quiet but blazing with the strength of the sun, just waiting for a chance at freedom. One only needs to lift the blanket of despair one final time to let the rays of her soul shine on this impending oblivion.

My life has prepared me for this moment. We all have our purposes. It's not always clear, but we need to understand we were made for a reason. No matter how grand or insignificant, how painful or joyous, no matter the icon of our faith — be it God, or gods, or yourself — we all have jobs to do in the reality of nature, and I intend to do my job to the fullest.

I feel certain this will be my last work of devotion. If it succeeds — if my dedication to God will help Nevaeh find her own faith in *something more*, in her purpose — I will be able to rest at peace in the embrace of my Lord.

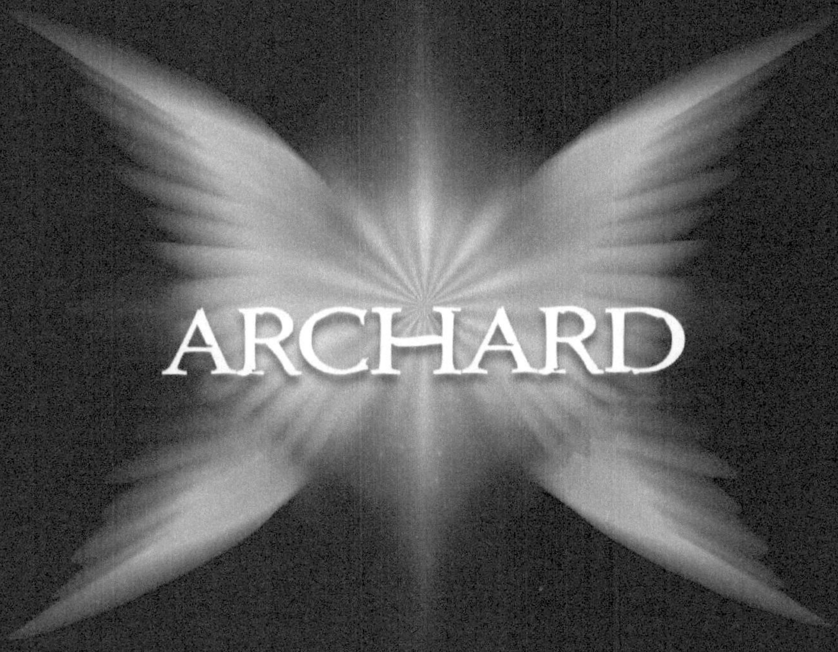
ARCHARD

CHAPTER TWENTY-THREE

THROUGH THE SILVERY WATERS

"Didn't I kill you once already?" I huffed, slamming Gavyn to the ground. Curling my back and broadening my shoulders, I readied myself to stampede the resurrected Celata.

Gavyn trundled onto his side, his face skewed with irritation and pain. He slung his fist toward me, releasing a ball of white-hot fire.

I ducked, digging my hooves into the ground. Snorting, I rushed him and angled my horns down, aiming for his ribs.

He tucked into a ball and rolled out of my path of destruction.

"You tried, but I guess you fail at everything you do," Gavyn spat, prowling in a slow semi-circle opposite me.

"Archard," Malach screamed, soaring anxiously above us. His wings turned up at the ends, and he dove for me.

His large hands hooked under my arms. We lifted into the air, heading toward the mirrored waters swirling next to the Hell portal.

I struggled in his grip, wanting to finish Gavyn. "Let me go! That asshole needs to be stopped. He'll ruin everything."

"Jacan took her into the Heavens," was all the explanation he gave.

My eyes fell to the floor, where I'd pinned Nevaeh before Gavyn made his appearance. She was gone. Jacan was gone. My Ophanim was gone.

I relaxed my face, allowing its transformation back to my usual human-like shape. "Arkin. Go back. We need him," I told Malach. "We need everyone we can get. If they have Vanna, they'll be able to open the gates."

A disapproving growl exploded from Malach's chest, but he steered left and dipped toward the ground.

"Arkin," I yelled as we flew closer.

He planted his ax in a Crucio's skull then glanced up at me questioningly.

"Grab on!"

When we were within reach, Arkin flexed his wings, leaping into the air to meet us. He locked his hand around my forearm, and I locked mine around his.

"A little help would be nice," Malach scoffed, peering down at me.

Clutching a handful of his leather vest, I threw out all four of my wings, thrusting upward. My power of flight surpassed Malach's, and I assumed the lead, flying us toward the Heaven portal.

"You sure this will work, Mal?" Arkin asked, doubtful.

"Just hold onto me. We should all be able to get through. Jacan carried the others in."

"Yeah, but—"

Before Arkin finished his concerned protest, I jetted us all through the silvery waters.

Time slowed, its effects resembling a tractor-trailer hitting a brick wall at full speed.

I sucked in a loud, deep breath as we broke through the other side.

My lungs filled with the Glory I'd missed for so many years. I felt like a fish, beached for far too long, finally making it back to the sea. My skin prickled. My heart thudded with what seemed like the first beat it had pumped since I'd left.

I stopped flapping my wings, overcome by entering the portal for the first time in decades. Below me, Arkin gasped, likely feeling the same sensations I was.

Malach pushed upward, picking up my slack to drag Arkin and I into the secondary portal.

Once we made it across, Malach released us. My back and heels smacked the ground. I grimaced from the pain shooting through my legs into my spine. Arkin groaned, his backside hitting the lush grass next to me.

I propped myself up on my elbow, gritting my teeth from the pang of soreness zooming up my back. Widening my eyes, I smiled and relished the magnificence that was the spirit sky. Millions of human souls sparkled from their orbs of happy eternity, lighting up the colorful backdrop of God's power.

It was breath-taking...just as I remembered.

"Open the fucking gates," a dark tone demanded from the North. "I know you can do it, so open them. I'll kill him, I promise. Then that blood will be on your hands, Ophanim."

"Vanna," I exhaled, regret and pity layering her name.

Malach landed beside us, perching his fists on his hips. His eyes narrowed in their direction. "They're at the gate. Jacan has his scepter pointed at the Principality kneeling at his feet. The other Dominion is pressing the Ophanim against the gates. Nevaeh's just standing there, watching. Waiting, it looks like."

"What are we gonna do?" Arkin asked quietly.

I shook my head. "I don't know. The only thing we can do, I guess." My eyes roamed over the landscape around us, wishing I had more time to enjoy it. "We fight. Like we always do. Like we've always done." I paused for a beat, swallowing my pride and my love for Nevaeh. "We have to kill them. Kill her. It's the only way."

Lowering my gaze, I focused on a single blade of impossibly-green grass. The heat of Malach's attention bore into me, but I knew he understood it was the only option.

Arkin smoothed his hand over my shoulder and squeezed. "I'm with ya, brother. Whatever you think is necessary, we'll do it together."

The cold breath of evil blew over my skin. I shivered, twisting to look at the portal behind us. Three Aether demons howled in delight as they traversed into angel territory.

HAVEN CAGE

CHAPTER TWENTY-FOUR

OPEN THE GATES

"They're coming," I said. "The demons are making it through. It won't be much longer."

The eerie squalling and spine-tingling maliciousness of the Aethers came hurling toward us.

Their evil laid over me like taffy—thick, sticky, and so sweet. It soothed my turmoil, offering me a reminder of who I'd grown to be after I left this place, a jolt of the fearless being I'd often wavered from since I'd taken over Neveah's body.

The Aethers drifted around us, disfigured phantoms riding the wind while awaiting their orders.

Jacan yelled at the Ophanim, "This is your last warning! Open the gates, Vanna. The Principality won't be the only angel dying if you don't. Think about where that will leave your precious God, then. One of His Wheels decimated to ashes. Who will guard Him then? Who will uphold his throne?" He abandoned the Principality, realizing the threat of a lesser angel wouldn't be enough.

Stomping in behind the Ophanim, Jacan shoved his partner out of the way. He spread his fingers along the top of Vanna's smooth head and mashed her face into the bars separating us from the kingdom beyond. Leaning in next to her ear, his body pushing into hers, he whispered, "You don't want to die, do you?"

As he made his intentions to harm her clear, a shade of blood and soot crept up the tips of his flight feathers. A strained moan broke from his throat.

He was losing his Holiness. Soon, he wouldn't be able to turn back. Soon, he'd be like me, so consumed by anger and hate for our maker that he'd morph into something more powerful than those bound by the strings of God.

"Jacan," his partner called, guardedly. His saucer-sized eyes were pinned to the darkness slithering into his leader's wings.

"What?" Jacan snarled. Spittle flung from his lips, pelting Vanna in one of her many watchful orbits.

"Your...your wings," he stuttered, "they're changing."

"Wasn't that the plan, you dim-wit?" He turned his body toward the other Dominion, keeping a firm hand jammed against the Ophanim's back. "Did you think we could come out of this, betraying Father, and still get to keep the power He gave us? Did you think we'd go unpunished?" Jacan shook his head. "You were severely misinformed if that was the case. Think about what freedom we'll be gaining in return, brother."

Jacan's second-in-command tore his gaze from the stained feathers. A frown pulled at his mouth as he considered his leader's proposal. He looked at the gates, a hint of regret sliding across his features, before he nodded once and hardened his posture.

"Now, where was I?" Jacan purred, leaning his body back into Vanna.

"The only time you'll walk past these gates again is when you are succumbing to judgment."

Jacan's shoulders trembled around a hearty laugh. He peeked over the ridge of his wings to find me observing his actions with interest. "The only one who can judge is on my side, Ophanim. I don't think I have to worry about that." Sliding a rigid hand up her neck and along her face, he positioned each one of his digits over one of her eyes. She shrieked as he drove his nails into five of her eyeballs. Blood oozed around his fingers. The red droplets trickled down her cheeks, contrasting with her porcelain skin.

Vanna grunted and bucked away from the bars. Her head snapped back, bashing Jacan's face with a loud thwack.

Jacan wobbled then stumbled to the ground. Pinching the bridge of his bleeding nose, he pointed his scepter toward the Ophanim. A white energy orb blasted from the tip.

Before the orb hit Vanna, she threw up her arms. The translucent bands of power that always rotated around her flashed to solid spinning strips protecting her. The orb deflected off her guard and fizzled out.

Growling, Jacan slapped the grass, hoisted himself up, then slashed his scepter through the air. Another white ball of energy landed squarely on the Principality's chest. The lesser angel dropped like a sack of flour.

Vanna screamed. Tears erupted from each of her glossy eyes. Her forehead rested against the inside of her protective bubble as she sobbed for her lost friend.

"Enough," I yelled. "I will get the gates to open, one way or another."

Raising my hands, I scoured the souls inside me and reached for Layla's essence. My mind wrapped around a tendril of her gift. I yanked hard, bringing the ability forward.

I chanted the command appropriate for my Aethers to understand and slung my hands outward.

The phantoms broke their spiraling formation in the sky, racing toward the gates. The bars vibrated with a low *pong* from their impact but didn't budge.

"Son of a bitch," I shouted, calling the demons back to me. My sights fell on the sobbing Ophanim. Allowing my eyes to unfocus, I could see a slight quaver in the invisible shield encompassing her. I slowly scrubbed my hands together, a thought of coercion forming in my mind. I ran my tongue along my teeth then smiled.

Chanting, I grabbed at the Aethers' reins and slung my hands toward Vanna, waiting for her shield to crumble under the demons' invasion.

She might be able to uphold her powers with us, but the subtle ripple in her protective shield said she was damaged. I wondered if she'd be able to withstand demons, less dense than the air, piercing her glorious bubble.

As the phantoms darted toward their target, a figure swooped in front of Vanna.

Archard bounced up from his landing crouch, his wings spreading out to guard the Ophanim.

Echoing thuds announced the Guardian, Arkin, and Jacan's second sparring to my left.

A *humph*, followed by Jacan yelling, "Kill him! Kill them all, dammit," drew my eyes to the night sky. Malach hefted the Dominion higher and higher, engaging him in an aerial war.

I ground my teeth and exhaled fury through my nostrils. I snapped my fingers, tightening them into white-knuckled fists. I readied Nevaeh's beast for attack, gathering its rampant power in my mental grasp.

Lowering my gaze to Archard, I noticed the swarm of Aethers dodge Archard and Vanna. They made a hard turn in my direction.

Repeating Layla's chant louder, I attempted to regain control of the demons.

High-pitched cackling rang in my head while the demons barreled toward me.

Uh-oh. Poor Master. The title was laced with revulsion and defiance. *I'm going to rip you to pieces with those Aethers, you bastard. I don't care if it's the last thing I do,* Layla promised in my mind.

I backed up a step, but it was too late.

Searing pain spiked through me like a spear as the first demon sifted into my thigh. I toppled backward, smacking my head on the ground. Dizziness sloshed the thoughts around in my skull. I blinked, reaching for the little bit of focus I had.

Clenching my jaw shut, I raised up on my elbows and glared at Nevaeh's Guardian. I hurled myself to the side, evading another Aether.

Expelling a grunt of frustration, I yanked my fists into my sides tight, pulling Nev's cloud of doom in to act as my defense. Masses of thick clouds churned in a slow cyclone, clinging to me like armor.

I sprang up, standing in the darkness, sensing the beings outside of my pitch-black storm. Aiming my focus for Archard, I shot a bolt of torrid energy from my fingers. The violet streak arced from me, zapping my target in a continuous flow of deadly power.

Marching forward, I bid the beast to clear a path from me to Nevaeh's angel. I wanted to see the life fade from his eyes. I wanted him to know it would be *me*, Rhett, stealing his soul when his physical form expired.

Archard convulsed, slumping backward into the Ophanim's spinning sphere. She beat against the inside, a canary caged from the world crumbling before her eyes.

My bolt followed him down, slamming his body violently against the ground.

"Stop," Vanna cried. "Nevaeh, stop this." Her multitude of eyes darted up to me, begging for mercy.

"I'm. Not. Nevaeh," I gritted.

"Can't you see what you're letting happen? Do something." The Ophanim pounded her palm against her bands, her expression twisted in desperation.

"Oh, I see it alright," I responded with a grin. Panting, I cinched off my power. I didn't want him completely dead. *Yet.*

I squatted down next to Archard, slapping his cheek hard enough to rouse some sense of consciousness in him. His eyeballs rolled down from the back of his skull. They roamed aimlessly in his sockets until he was able to settle them on my face and maintain concentration.

"Don't let the lights go out too early, my friend. You'll miss my victory dance on the other side of those pearly gates." I nudged my chin toward the gleaming barricades.

"Nevaeh," Vanna prayed, "please, child, please come back to us." The Ophanim dropped to her knees, her hands sliding down, inches from Archard's shoulder.

Ignoring her prayer, I asked, "You ready to open those gates now?"

Her lips trembled. She shook her head much slower than before, less adamant in her answer. She was debating the consequences. Realizing her hope was in vain.

"Is it worth losing him over?" I pushed. "You could have the same freedom as us."

Her eyes narrowed, glowering up at me. Those heart-shaped lips curled back into a hate-filled sneer. "I don't want the freedom you offer, Devil. I rebuke your promises. I rebuke your existence."

With the snap of my fingers, I ejected another flare of power, shocking Archard's heart.

"No, no, no!" She screamed in a rush.

I cocked an eyebrow and smirked, waiting for her to take the bait.

She exhaled a quivering breath, strings of spit gathering in the corner of her angry mouth. Quietly, she submitted. "Okay."

Leaning in closer, I knitted my brows together, pretending I didn't hear her defeat. "I...I'm sorry. Did you say something?"

GEORGE

CONFESSIONS OF A LOST SOUL

Never, in all my years before Nevaeh, did I expect to be a part of such a grim future.

I feel like I've already died a thousand deaths, but God kept giving me breath. Keeping me here for some reason I couldn't fathom.

A piece of me died when I lost my pa as a boy. Another piece went when my ma didn't make it home from the hospital the summer of '68.

Part of me chipped away when I gave up on myself and surrendered to self-pity, wallowing about the things I couldn't change in my life.

Then, when my poor Bonnie and sweet Anna fell victim to my demons, I said, "That's it. There's nothing left to take."

I just wandered around, barely keeping myself alive, for years. A zombie, I suppose. Hollow to the core. All my troubles had dug me from the inside out and left me without anything to live for.

Rottin' in the dirt seemed like a fine alternative after all that.

When Nev ended up under that dock, it was like that damn heart of mine ran into an electric fence and started pumpin' for the first time in years.

The love that came with that first beat was the first bit of warmth I'd felt in my old bones since losing my Anna.

That lost little girl saved me. She showed me that life was worth sticking around for. Nev showed me I was worth forgiving. She became my reason to live. My daughter.

Now, the world is drowning. Seems it wouldn't make a difference to me, since I'm dead, but the Good Lord has given me another chance to redeem myself. One of these days, there will most definitely be an end to my luck, but until then, I will make her see.

I will make her see her worth.

I will give her the same love she offered me. I'll fill her heart with strength and love like she did mine.

CHAPTER TWENTY-FIVE

CAN YOU FEEL HOW RIGHT THIS IS?

I had her.

"Okay, I'll open the gate," Vanna rasped, her head hanging in defeat.

I slapped my thighs and hopped up. Swinging my hands out in half-circles, as if I was pushing curtains aside, the beast vanished from the immediate area, allowing me a clear view of the other angels.

Malach and Jacan plummeted toward the ground, trading punches along the way. They spun like a top, battling for control over flight and will.

Arkin was beating the other Dominion to a pulp, bloodying his face with the handle of his ax.

They were useless. Their ability to help me had ended the moment we made it to the Heavens.

I angled my head, contemplating Vanna. She was all I needed now.

Stepping over Archard's dying body, I approached the gate. "Sometime today, Ophanim. I've waited long enough for this." My blood pulsed in rapid *whomp, whomp, whomps* in my ears.

The foreign undercurrent of power emitted by the gates sparked to life the closer I got to the towering spindles. I curled a hand around one of the looped rods, soaking up the buzz of Holiness singing in the metal.

A flourish of gold writing shimmered in reaction, rippling over my knuckles to swim down the inside of my palm. Giggling in fascination, I studied the slants and slopes of the letters, recognizing them as my own.

Everything had come full-circle. It was meant to be. It was always meant to be my revolution, not hers.

I could feel the Clavis's gift tingling beneath my skin, anxious to unlock the mysteries of Heaven to me once again.

"Do you feel it?" I questioned, turning my head to look at Vanna. "Can you feel how right this is?"

She choked out a disbelieving laugh. "Nothing about this is right, traitor."

Fresh rage chilled my heart. I pointed a finger toward Archard and zapped him with a quick bolt of energy, determined to make her obey. "You'll see. Once it's all said and done. You'll see how wrong you were. Now, give me your fucking hand."

She sniveled, biting back more sobs as she searched Archard's abused body for signs of life.

"Don't worry, he's still alive, but one more hit of my fury…" I let my words trail off. There was no need to finish; she understood me with crystal clarity.

Vanna inhaled deeply then exhaled the last of her resolve. Her shoulders fell along with her shield. The spinning bands softened, fading to a barely-visible state.

Sliding closer to the gates, she hunched over, staring at the ground, and lifted an unsteady hand.

I grabbed her wrist, jerking it the last three inches to connect her with the barrier standing in my way.

Light as bright as the sun erupted under our hands. I squinted, craning my neck away. The gates began to shudder, rattling my bones so hard I thought they might splinter.

This was it.

I'd waited decades for this chance.

My freedom was just on the other side, and I was about to claim it.

There was a victorious give in the bars. They set into motion, unraveling from their maze of loops and swirls, clearing a way for me to cross into the angelic spheres.

Pure elation filled my body. My eyes widened, stunned by the gates of God unlocking to my will.

As I impatiently waited for the last shackle of my imprisonment to fall, a torrent of voices filled my mind. Images of a life not my own filtered into my vision, holding me hostage in my head.

HAVEN CAGE

NEVAEH

CHAPTER TWENTY-SIX

MAKE OUR DEATHS MEAN SOMETHIN'

Nevaeh, Layla shouted. *Dammit, get your shit together, and put your big-girl panties on.*

Gauzy still-shots of a lanky boy with years of pain and suffering etched on his face flashed before me. It was Dominic, Layla's brother.

Please, don't leave him alone. Bring him back. You have to give him the life I couldn't. Don't let this asshole bury you so deep you disappear, Nev. This is your body. Your gifts.

Layla's plea drenched me in sorrow, fear, and regret. The greatest of her emotions, though, was determination.

More ghostly stills, of Dominic and Father Varga, faded in. New emotions—humility, adoration, and conviction—mingled with Layla's.

The phrase, *have faith, sister*, echoed around me in a thick European accent. *You are enough*, Father Varga assured. *The remorse and agony caged within your soul is enough. It polishes your tarnished heart. Believe in Him. Believe in your abilities. Believe in yourself.*

He showed me memories of a grand church, emanating a sense of peace I'd only felt when embraced in Archard's arms.

In a following image, a younger version of himself assumed the position of leader, teacher, father, and friend among his fellow sinners. He carefully pulled a long black garment over his head, smoothing gentle hands over the creases as it brushed the floor.

Unmistakable fulfillment sparkled in his blue eyes. Father Varga was complete, content, to serve his maker. It shone through the ritualistic manner in which he draped his vestments along his stout body.

Nevaeh, my girl. George's voice engulfed me like the heat of a campfire on a cold winter night.

I reached out for him from my dark prison, needing his hug, his comfort.

Memories we'd shared together, as father and daughter, flipped through my conscience. Snaps of us playing in the rain because we had nowhere else to go to stay dry, huddling under a worn blanket when I was sick with the flu, and George watching me braid my hair before a job hunt, stacked on top of Layla's and Father Varga's spate of shimmering images. In each vision, George wore an expression of unconditional love.

The sensation of his essence folded around me, consoling my sullen spirit as if he were there, pulling me into his side for one of his long bear-hugs.

I never thought our adventure together would lead us here...but it did, girlie. I'd do it all again, ya know...take all the pain and loss to have you as my daughter. As much as I'd love to have my Bonnie and Anna, you are just as important to me. You reminded me what it was like ta live again. You saved me from a lonely life, Nevaeh. It's time to do what you were made for. It's time to save the others.

"But I didn't save you," I cried. "You're dead. You're *all* dead."

Yeah, but you can make our deaths mean somethin', George said. *If you allow Rhett to bury you in a coffin of yer own flesh an' blood, we died for nothin'. And, what about them men? The ones ya loved? Will you give him the chance to take their lives in vain too?*

The glimmer of a new picture sifted through the rest. Gavyn was in the factory fighting the Guardians.

He's alive, Nev, Layla said. *You could save him from the damned eternity I helped create for him.*

"What?" I whispered to myself, eyeing the image of Gavyn with a heavy heart. "Archard killed him, though."

Hell needed a master. I guess, when Rhett managed to leave in your body, Gav was the next best thing.

Gavyn's frame vanished, and Archard, laying on the ground with his eyes closed, appeared.

The angel doesn't have much time either, Nevaeh. Father Varga's words were full of sympathy. *The portals are consuming the human realm, the angelic chains are broken, souls are hanging in limbo, and Rhett is standing at the opened gates of Heaven. I know it's a lot to accept, but you are the only one who can stop this.*

I thought about what they told me, sorting through visions of a lost Gavyn and a dying Archard. My heart was tearing in two, begging me to do something to save *them*, if nobody else. The two men had captured the most guarded piece of me and unknowingly played tug-o-war with it through the last several fucked-up months.

I'd tried my damnedest to deny who I was, only to be forced into my fate anyway. Then, I lost myself totally in the shadows of a monster. Sadly, *I* was the monster. Rhett was just one hell of a puppeteer. He merely used the darkness in me to carry out his devious plans.

Whether I did the damage myself, or someone used my power to commit the destruction, it all came down to me being the wicked one.

I cowered in a whirlwind of guilt, shame, defeat, and dread, wishing we had never stepped foot in Joe's.

Don't do that, Nev, George urged. *Don't fade inside yerself. This is the road we took, and there's no turning back. You know we would'a ended up here one way or another. It was always gonna be you, kid.* There was a breath of pensive silence while he let his words soak in. *God wouldn't have chosen you if he didn't think you could shoulder this burden.*

My conscience zeroed in on flashes of Gavyn struggling with the same chain of blood that had tethered Bron to the underworld. In the background, cut and bruised angels fought demons breaching the veils, while unconscious Dominions littered the factory floor.

Surrounding the warring beings were two holes, one edged in scourging fire and one ringed by violently swirling water. Both were battling for claim on the factory's spatial existence. I could barely see the four-story-high cinderblock walls or the iron beams supporting the ceiling.

A foreign voice called my name, tearing me from the apocalyptic scene running through my mind. "Nevaeh," she repeated, desperate for my attention. "Please, stop him. You can't let him pass the gates."

I blinked, shocked by the melodious sound of her words. The sheer vision of Gavyn and the Guardians vanished, replaced by a magnificent creature with eyes dotting her beautiful face.

She stared at me, terror and gloom clouding each deep pupil.

I sucked in air as if it were the first time I'd breathed in days. I hadn't realized how far down he'd stuffed me. I hadn't been able to see or hear the outside world since he assumed control at the mine.

My eyes roamed from the strange creature begging me for help to the intricate bars sliding against one another, clearing the area in front of me for passage.

I craned my head, distracted by the endless dark sky over-head. It glittered with peculiar stars bobbing on brightly-colored waves of light.

A loud roar alerted me to a scuffle speeding toward me. My gaze darted to the left.

Malach delivered a hard blow to Jacan's jaw.

The two warriors cork-screwed, flying along the ground with their wings scraping up clumps of dirt and grass as they fought to be on top. Finally, Malach placed a hand on either side of Jacan's head and jerked upward, driving him into a cracked urn-like object floating in mid-air.

Jacan's eyes closed, his head drooping to the side. Malach let go of the Dominion, not caring where he landed.

I turned, hearing heavy panting behind me. Arkin bent at the waist, braced by his hands on his knees. Satisfied the angel at his feet would stay on the ground, passed out, he lifted his gaze. Arkin scowled at me under an angry brow.

I held up my palms to protest the accusation in his eyes, but his figure blurred then faded to black. I stumbled backward, disoriented by the sudden loss of sight.

You're not going to mess this up for me. I'm stronger than you, Rhett scorned. *I'm too fucking close.*

His will beat down on me like a ton of dirt trapping me in a bottomless grave.

In the distance, I heard Layla, Father Varga, and George calling my name. They encouraged me, each in their own way, offering their determination, faith, and love to build my strength. Their emotions were a breath of fresh air while Rhett tried to suffocate me with his horrible intentions.

Digging deep within myself, I reached for tendrils of the endowments God instilled in me. The frayed strands of sizzling power and my parent's life-force tangled around my senses like yarn tangling around my fingers. They were just as eager to join with me as I was with them.

No…No, you don't deserve this. I was the one He chose. I'm a Holy being, dammit, Rhett protested. *I made the Clavis with my own hands and blood*, he whined.

Thick ribbons of influence and supremacy strapped around my wrists, glided up my arms, and banded around my heart. The power melted into my core, infusing me with the will of an all-knowing ruler.

I squeezed my eyes shut and surrendered myself—body, mind, and soul.

A torrent of energy rolled along my spine then surged outwards.

Rhett's protests died.

The other voices in my head calmed.

The ripple of energy discharged from my fingertips, toes, chest, and mouth in a blast that shook the atmosphere. When I opened my eyes, Malach and Arkin were launching backward in the air. They landed yards away, expelling grunts upon impact.

A hand clasped around my ankle, insisting I look down. Archard's pained gaze beamed up at me.

"Nevaeh?"

NEVAEH

HAVEN CAGE

CHAPTER TWENTY-SEVEN

SEAL THE PORTALS

Archard's grasp on my leg weakened. His hand thumped the ground. His aqua eyes fluttered shut.

I fell to my knees beside him, cupping my hands around his cheeks. Tears stung my eyes. I pressed my lips together to stop their trembling.

The strange woman with the head full of eyes knelt on the other side of Archard. Tears spilled down her face freely. If only I could permit my own tears the same freedom.

If I allowed myself to break, I'd never come back from it.

The pings and scraping of metal on metal ceased behind the woman, signaling the Heavenly gates were fully open.

The sharp, cool tip of a blade bit into the back of my neck, forcing me to freeze.

"Don't move," Malach gritted.

Arkin eased into my view, gripping his ax like it was his life-line. His nostrils flared. His cautious eyes scrutinized me.

"It's me…Nevaeh," I said, slowly raising my hands in surrender.

Malach dug his sword into my skin. Warm fluid dripped from the point of pinching pressure and soaked into the collar of my shirt. "I said don't move."

The many-eyed woman bent over Archard, raising her hand to the blade poised on my neck. Her glossy gaze drifted from me to Malach. "She speaks truth."

Arkin glanced at the woman then back at me, his stance relaxing a minute amount. "Even if she is. How long will she be Nev?" he asked warily.

"Surely, you understand we can't take that chance anymore," Malach added, lessening his sword's bite on my nape, yet keeping it trained on me.

Arkin's attention shifted to a spot I couldn't see. "Malach," he said, nudging his chin to the South.

Malach exhaled a loud, disheartened breath then lowered his weapon.

The eye-studded creature focused on the same spot Arkin examined and gasped.

I twisted on my shins and choked back a sob.

A seam of shimmering, hot embers rolled across the rich, grassy knoll of Heaven as wide as the eye could see. Behind the seam was a warped window into the Human realm. The demons and angels below paused their battles, realizing the realms were melting together. Once the Guardians noticed the covetous hunger in the demons' black eyes, they reanimated, fighting fiercer than I've ever seen them fight before.

They were defending their home.

Crouched in the middle of the chaos, Gavyn clutched the collar around his neck, tugging against its magical restraint. His face contorted under frustration and agony. He geared his attention toward the opening. His eyes landed on mine, and he stilled, the pain in his expression deepening.

Malach looked down at me, his jaw tensing as he pondered my true identity. After a brief moment, he settled on a decision and said, "We've got more work to do."

The tension and disbelief in his voice remained, but he didn't have many options. Time was slipping away, along with the boundaries of the realms.

"Nev, you have to seal the portals." Arkin squatted to my level. "If you are really her," he pleaded, bracketing my shoulders in his big hands and squeezing, "you'll seal them. Now."

I nodded, pushing myself up. I marched toward the line where Earth, Heaven, and Hell met. Holding my hands out, I reached for my beast, calling her to me. She cloaked me in a storm of power and protection, the way she was always meant to do.

With the burning embers approaching my toes, I stared down at Gavyn, remembering who he used to be. I scanned over the angels, thankful for their existence. I considered the demons, determined to put them back where they belonged. Then, I closed my eyes and pictured Archard. Homing in on his relentless faith in me, I opened my mouth, urging the notes to float up from my gut. They drifted out in an eerie song of love and hope. Of will and strength.

Heat from the encroaching rift soaked into my boots, forcing me to retreat a step. I belted out more of my song, praying that I had enough power to reverse the damage I'd caused.

"That's it, Nev. You're doing it," Arkin praised through the dense cover of sparking clouds. "Just a little more, and they'll be closed."

Opening my eyes, I watched the edge of Hell retract, leaving Heaven's lush ground in its wake. A few more notes shrunk the Holy portal to a manageable size—just big enough for a single body to get through. The Hell portal also shrank. Their borders were separated, their conjoined power short-circuited. None of the demons would make it through without my help. And I wouldn't be doing that anytime soon.

I commanded my cloud up, so it hovered a foot above my head, spinning in a lazy hurricane. Biting back a shriek of amazement, I surveyed the grandeur of gleaming fence-lines on either side of the opening into Heaven's Glory.

"The Hell portal?" Malach asked, the edge of vigilance clear in his question.

"I'll close it, but I have some business to tend to first." Every one of those demons were going back today. My heart ached at the realization, I would have to send Gavyn back as well. And Rhett would most certainly go back. I'd make sure of it, if I had to spend the rest of my pathetic life figuring out how I'd manage to keep him there.

A soul-quaking cry echoed through the air.

"Vanna," Arkin breathed, turning to face the woman with many-eyes.

Shaking my head, I corrected him, "It's Archard. He's hurt." I sprinted to my angel, sliding to a stop on my knees at his head.

"He's...he's dying," Vanna whimpered. She rocked back and forth, her hands clasped in prayer over her heart.

"No," I argued in denial. "No, he's hurt, but he'll be okay." I peered up at Malach, searching his worried eyes for confirmation. "He'll be okay, right?" My words came out in a high-pitched whine I didn't recognize. An acute ache staked its claim in my heart when Malach didn't respond.

I combed stray locks of Archard's golden hair back from his face, then slid my hands down his temples. Smoothing gentle lines along the beautiful contours of his cheekbones, I begged, "Wake up, please. Archard, you've finally gotten me back, don't leave now."

His eyelids remained closed, but he parted his lips. "The Tran...sender."

"Wha...?" I trailed off in confusion, my brows knitting together as I searched the other angels for clarification. "What's he saying?"

"He's talking about the Soul Bearer's Transcender," a female answered over my shoulder.

My head snapped toward the familiar voice. Narrowing my eyes, I drank in her long, dark hair pinned back in a cascade of curls. Her almond-shaped eyes matched my mother's, but her chin was slightly smaller, and her nose tipped up a degree more, like mine.

"Grandma?"

"Nice to see you again, Theora," Malach greeted, pulling her in for a hug.

Arkin took her hand in his and patted it, sharing a heart-felt smile.

"Repair...the Transcend...er," Archard grunted.

"I don't understand," I muttered, frustrated.

Malach wandered to the urn-like structure hanging in the air. "It's cracked." He dragged a hand around the bottom of it, then looked at me. "This is how you deliver souls to the Heavens."

I coughed out a disbelieving laugh. With so much that had happened, I really hadn't thought of what I would do with the souls I held. Using the white-marble urn Malach was stroking to facilitate my efforts in divvying souls out was hard for me to imagine.

Archard's hand rested on mine, grabbing my attention. "Use...me."

"You're not making any sense," I whispered, leaning down to kiss his forehead.

"Perfect sense," Vanna chimed. "He carried God's throne. He can carry souls."

Theora sucked in a breath of understanding and cupped a hand over her mouth. She eyed the Transcender for a moment, then spoke. "The Holiness I gave him...hopefully, he has enough left."

"Come on, people. Lay it out for me," I barked. "What do I need to do to save him?"

"Not...save. Use," Archard sputtered.

Arkin lowered to one knee and hung his head. "Son of a bitch," he exhaled. "He's saying he wants you to take his soul. Use it to power the Transcender. He can carry the souls to their eternities because he was made for carrying God's Glory. He's a Cherubim. Transporting and guarding is their purpose."

My mouth dropped open, stuck on words that refused to come out.

How could he propose something like that? What would it mean for his future? For *our* future? We'd gone through so much. For him to leave me now...for him to *choose* to leave me.

A thousand tiny fissures splintered on the surface of my heart.

Bowing around my tightening chest, I leaned down and kissed Archard. His lips were cool, his breath unsteady against my face.

He winced, dragging his hand up to curl around the back of my neck. "If I'm going to die, my love...this is how...I want to meet my afterlife...with purpose and splendor."

A wretched sound, one of loss and denial, escaped my swollen throat in a wail. Tears reached my brim, spilling down my cheeks unforgivingly.

"I can't do this, Archard. Please, don't make me do this."

I kissed him again, skimming my fingers over his hair then down his neck to rest on his chest. I sensed the life draining from his body.

His faint pulse and closed eyes slammed me into the realization that I wouldn't be leaving Heaven with Archard today.

NEVAEH

HAVEN CAGE

CHAPTER TWENTY-EIGHT

GOODBYE

Arkin kept his head bowed as he mumbled his goodbyes to Archard. "Thank you. Thank you for always standing by me. For watching my back." His head rolled up, and he looked at my grandmother, smiling sweetly. "For showing me that love is worth the risk. That it's worth breaking the confines of our beliefs and comfort." Arkin sniffled, tearing his gaze from Theora.

His brow pinched together, his mouth turning down in sadness. "Thank you for being more than my brother in battle. Thank you for being my brother in heart and soul." Pressing the heels of his palms into his glossy eyes, he shoved up to his feet. With his tears staunched, he lowered his hands and prayed, "I wish your spirit an eternity of happiness and fulfillment."

Arkin turned his back to us, wandering aimlessly away.

Malach genuflected next to me, laying a hand on Archard's shoulder. "If anyone deserves the admirable fate of relinquishing souls to their afterlives, it's you, my friend. Always finding a way to break the rules for a noble cause." A weak smile tugged at his lips. "May you have an eternity of contentment in your holy servitude. I hope we meet again one day."

Malach glanced at me, offering a sympathetic nod. When I reacted with wide eyes and a shaking head, he smoothed his hand over my hair. His comforting gesture did little to calm the reluctance in my heart. "You are the Soul Bearer, now. Deal his judgement, and put him to rest, Nevaeh." The Archangel bent forward and kissed my forehead, then stood.

He walked toward Jacan's unconscious body, hefting him over his shoulder, before trudging to Jacan's accomplice. Malach squatted and fisted the back of the accomplice's shirt. He escorted the traitorous angels through the gates, the trio disappearing the moment they crossed the threshold.

My grandma's hand brushed the width of my shoulders as she knelt beside me. A tear slipped from her eye, following the bridge of her nose until it bumped the peak of her lip. She licked it away. "I know it's hard, baby. It's what he wants, though. Don't let the pain in your heart keep him from his destiny."

She caressed Archard's cheek, the compassion and love she'd always been known for shining down on him. "Peace, Archard. I'll visit you every day."

She lifted her hand from Archard's cheek and rested it on mine, urging me to look her in the eyes. They were the blue of the cleanest lake on the clearest day. An abundance of goodness danced behind them, consoling my sullen soul for a fraction of time. "I'll see you when it's your turn. Until then, I'll be watching you."

My grandmother rose to her feet. She skirted around Archard and Vanna, making her way through the gates behind Malach.

Vanna and I looked at each other with a somber curiosity. I didn't know anything about this creature, but it was plain to see she had deep ties to Archard's past. The heartbreak racking her body mimicked my own.

We were sisters in grief. We shared a love for this angel, and I couldn't deny her closure any more than I'd deny it for myself.

Her multitude of eyes lowered to Archard's slack face. Her mind churning over what I assumed were precious memories of their life together.

"Our connection was a thing of our Father's. It was ancient and sturdy. We loved each other because it was right. We were a blessed pair."

Though I knew Archard's feelings for me were true, it still hurt to hear someone else had experienced his love like I had.

Her gaze drifted to my face. Her perfect mouth curved in a smile. "What you have is something new. It is soul-binding. You are two parts of one." She blinked, studying my trembling lips. "Unpredictable. Unrelenting. Indestructible."

Her smile fell, a trace of...was that jealousy...bled through her sorrow. "He was forever yours."

She dipped down, whispering her private goodbye in Archard's ear.

Vanna rose, turning for the gates.

I grabbed her wrist. "Won't you stay?" The question tumbled out in an anxious jumble.

"I have my own duties to attend," she answered indifferently.

Releasing her arm, I dropped my hands in my lap, feeling lost. "I...I don't know how to do this." I turned my head, studying the Transcender. The shiny, white surface was marked by skinny black lines, jagged and endless like the cracks in my heart.

"He'll show you the way," she assured. Vanna left me alone with my misery.

Staring down at my Guardian, I memorized every single ridge, curve, and dip of his face. I traced my fingers over his soft skin, wanting to crawl inside him and never let him go.

His four wings fanned out over the ground, the white of them more vibrant and pure than I'd remembered.

I wiped my tears away using the back of my hand, then carefully moved his arm. Lowering to his side, I rested my head in the crook of his shoulder, soaking in the feel of his silky feathers under my back.

Snuggling against his ribs, I draped my leg over his and clung to him as if I could keep him here by mere touch. A labored inhale pulled at his chest. I buried my face in his shoulder and wept. The anguish consuming me shook both our bodies.

One final breath wheezed from his lungs.

I squeezed my eyes shut, lamenting the soul that was severed from mine. The pain struck me so deeply, I couldn't make a noise. I couldn't even find solace in an outburst of rage.

Damn him.

Damn me. If it hadn't been for me, Rhett wouldn't have used my gifts and killed Archard. He'd still be alive.

Flickers of light filtered through my eyelids, stealing me from thoughts of pity and dismay. I opened my eyes to find a shroud of black clouds hovering around us like a slow fog. Amethyst lightning crackled, leaping from one fluffy mass to another in quick, zig-zagged arcs.

I craned my neck, watching the light-show with mild appreciation. My beast was drawing close, offering comfort and a necessary nudge to do what I had to do.

Grazing my fingers over Archard's temples, I found the courage to focus. My lightning shot faster and discharged brighter when I connected with his memories.

I gasped.

Phantom images of *me* sprang up everywhere along the inside of our dome of dense clouds. It was a play-back of over two decades of my past with Archard. Pictures of him, while we were separated, showed his constant trials of searching for me. His soul was marked by self-beratement, repentance, fidelity, and desire. Every notch of time exuded his eternal love to God, and to me — even in his not-so-righteous moments.

I sat up, marveling in the magnitude of depth and beauty pouring from this man's…this angel's… soul.

Memories of his life before me swam amid those after me. He was so magnificent, it was physically hard to look at. Archard shone bright, embodying a Holiness I couldn't wrap my head around. He would be joyous in any position serving his creator, whether it was by tending God's throne…protecting me…or delivering souls to their resting places.

I peered down at his peaceful expression.

The ache in my chest began to lessen. I'd had my time with him, though it was short, but he was born to mend the bridge between me and the Heavens.

Sliding my hand up his neck, I tipped his jaw toward me and tenderly pressed my lips into his. Using my mouth, I opened him up to me and inhaled.

His essence flowed into me, easy and willing. It glided over my tongue and down my throat, leaving behind the delicious taste of Archard as it swam to that place where the other souls waited.

The transaction only took seconds. My beast lifted her cover on us. Star light and the glow stemming from the gates illuminated the atmosphere once more.

I jerked away from Archard's form, feeling him change under my fingertips. The solidity of his body softened to a blurry haze until it evaporated, leaving no remanence of him behind. It reminded me of the tiny feather I'd seen on the window after Archard came to visit George in Gavyn's apartment.

It was a shame so much beauty disappeared without a trace in the end.

I rolled up off the ground and forced myself to approach the Transcender. Eyeing the floating object wearily, I cleared my head, hoping pages of an instruction manual would flash through my mind.

Nevaeh, Archard reverberated in my head.

I half chuckled, half cried, overcome by elation to hear his voice one last time.

I didn't want to leave without telling you…I love you.

"I know," I said, grinning. "I love you too."

The sensation of his soul hugging me from the inside flooded me.

Now, concentrate and transfer me to the Transcender, he urged. *There are a lot of poor spirits down there waiting for you to harvest them.*

Accepting the fact that I still had so much ahead of me, I nodded and asked, "How do I transfer you?"

"Breathe into the base of it."

I jumped, startled by the person answering in Archard's place. Arkin stepped up to the Transcender, winking at me, a glimpse of his usual fun-loving self peeked through his sadness.

"Right," I said, feeling like I somehow knew that already. "Goodbye, Archard," I whispered, choking back more tears.

After one deep breath in, I positioned my mouth under the open base and blew out.

Archard's essence drifted from me in a bright tendril of vapor, then floated into the bottom of the marble urn. He swirled inside the hollow structure a few times, like wine spiraling in a flute, then settled against the wall of it.

Arkin and I looked at each other, waiting for something big to happen to signal everything was as it should be.

"Do you think it worked?" I asked Arkin, mesmerized by the flaring glow of my angel.

He shrugged. "Only one way to find out."

MALACH

CHAPTER TWENTY-NINE

BALANCING THE SPHERES

Jacan's weight bore down on me as I entered Heaven's doors. I propped his fellow-Dominion against my leg and readjusted Jacan on my shoulder. Hooking my fingers in the back of Gersham's shirt collar again, I dragged him deeper into the third angelic sphere.

I remembered Jacan's brother-in-treachery from times when I had entered the second sphere to obtain orders from angelic ranks higher than mine.

My gaze roamed over the domain of Heaven I called home. It was much like the natural landscapes in the Human realm, as was most otherworldly planes. There were always those differences, though.

Plants reached out for you to touch them like a puppy seeking praise. A soft glow lingered in the air, contrasting with a dark night sky speckled by the spirit-stars; light and dark coexisted without taking from one another.

Marching farther toward my destination, the constant thrum of divine energy vibrated in my bones, another difference from the Earthly plane. You could feel it anywhere in Heaven, but the higher the sphere you were in, the more magnified the thrum.

The angels stationed in the higher levels were less human-like as well. I assumed that was attributed to many reasons — duties, nearness to God's power, absence of interaction with human-life.

Bathing in the world I almost lost and all its mystical elements, I ventured closer to the invisible wall marking the end of one sphere and the beginning of another.

My skeleton nearly rattled loose once I was within two feet of the boundary. I stood stock-still, adjusting to the unsettling sensation until the rattle dulled to a slight jangle I could tolerate.

As I lifted my foot to step forward, someone called my name, halting my advance. I turned, squinting into the distance. Vanna trecked behind me, gaining ground quickly.

I waited for the unique angel, honored to be in her presence. It was a rare occasion for any of us below the third sphere to see an Ophanim. I'd graciously accept any chance to be in the company of a being so close to God's heart.

"I wasn't sure how long you'd be," I greeted with a smile as she neared.

"I wished him well many years ago. Wasn't a need to expound on his death. He will be imbedded in the grains of Father's glory again, so no sadness for that."

I nodded in agreement while scooting Jacan higher on my shoulder. "I suppose you will return to your station, now?"

Her eyes narrowed, shifting to Jacan. "I can't until the chain is mended. We'll put them back together."

She fisted the bunch of fabric I had in my right hand, taking Gersham's weight from my load. Widening her shoulders, she faced the boundary and stepped through.

There was a slightly murky shadow that appeared in the wall around her, a dimple in the shield. The boundary gave, permitting her passage, then wobbled like a soap-bubble until the break in energy evened back out.

I followed her, pressing into the flux of transcendent force marking the spheres' borders.

The landscape graduated from forests and gentle hills to large rocks and mountains covered in hearty vegetation.

She pulled Gersham up until he slumped against her body as if they were dancing. She fanned her free hand out in a quick waving gesture. Her bands of divine energy became visible, engulfing them both in a radiant spinning capsule.

Holding her prisoner tight, she floated off the ground. Vanna looked down at me from just above my head, her strange features lined with a trace of aggravation. "Coming?"

Flexing my shoulders, I threw my wings out and leaped for the sky. I flew behind her, towing Jacan to his rightful place.

We crossed miles of land, climbing to a higher elevation along the way. Vanna slowed, circling the tallest mountain in sight twice. The Ophanim pointed to a small cave in the side of a tall peak. It seemed high enough the stony point nearly pricked the starry night. "That will do," she said, scanning the area.

I drifted lower, following her into the slim opening, and tucked my wings in tight. Once we found our footing, I shoved Jacan from my shoulder, smirking when he crashed to the hard floor.

Tipping my head from side to side, I stretched my neck. "Well, we've got them back where they belong…how do we keep them here? We need to make sure they don't break the chain again."

Vanna raised her hand, pointing a finger at me.

I stared at her, confused about what she wanted me to do.

Suddenly, a rose-colored flame ignited at her knuckle. It grew, whipping past the tip of her nail, twirling around the digit ravenously.

She crouched, touching the flame to the junction where Jacan's stained wing met his back. He jolted awake, screaming in agony.

I gritted my teeth, imagining the pain he was in. I could almost sympathize with him. Then I remembered what he'd intended to do when he left his sphere and disregarded any pity I had.

Vanna operated quickly, cauterizing the flesh as she burned the wing from his body. The acrid smell of singed feathers wafted to my nose, forcing me to grimace.

I looked away, my gaze shifting to Gersham. He was awake, watching the Ophanim in silence. Fear and acceptance hollowed his expression. He knew what was coming. He knew this was the penance for his iniquities.

This was a necessary retribution for their sins.

Gersham wouldn't fight it like Jacan was. He'd found a morsel of humility since their plans had fallen to pieces.

After Vanna finished her task of disabling both Dominions, she stood, peering down at the bloody mess of plumes and bone. The two traitors remained on their knees, as they should've been, weeping at the loss of their freedom.

They still had the Holiness God gave them to keep the chain intact, but they lost what granted them freedom to roam their sphere. When we confiscated their scepters, their authority over the other angels would be eliminated too.

"We need another," Vanna said.

"I'll get whoever's left. Hopefully, the Guardians spared their miserable lives during the battle."

"One more will be enough to balance the sphere and shield the humans from Father's direct power."

Scrubbing my hands over my face, I prayed that there was at least one left in the factory.

I turned to exit the hole in the mountain, my wings swinging out to carry me off the ledge.

"Malach," Vanna called.

I paused, peering over my shoulder.

She lifted her eyes to the ceiling, tilting her head as if listening to something. "He has gifts for you to take back."

NEVAEH

CHAPTER THIRTY

Deliverance

"So, I just breathe them into the Transcender like I did with Archard?" I asked Arkin, my stomach twisting in nervous knots.

If I fucked this up somehow, would I be able to fix it? I couldn't bare another hitch in our attempts at righting the wrongs. My mental strength was two steps from its breaking point.

Arkin settled his hands on my shoulders, ducking to look straight into my eyes. "Listen, Nev. You have it in your blood. You got this. Trust in your God-given abilities. Trust in yourself, cupcake." His mouth quirked up in a half-smile.

I nodded without replying. He let go of me and stepped aside.

Turning into myself, I thought, *Father Varga?*

Whenever you are ready, he answered, excitement saturating his tone. *I've waited for this moment for a long time.*

I smiled at his willingness to trust me with his eternity.

Before I go, promise me something. He paused, waiting for me to agree. *Maybe not today, or tomorrow, but try to forgive yourself...one day.*

The notion made me cringe. How could I possibly forgive myself for nearly bringing the world to its end?

I'll try, I thought. *That's the best I can do.*

Let's go then, he urged. I imagined, if I could see him at that moment, his face would be lit up with rapture.

I leaned in, releasing a deep exhale into the bottom of the Transcender. Father Varga's spirit snaked out of my mouth and glided into the center of the hollowed marble.

Archard's essence closed in around Father Varga, surrounding it in a globe of light.

The globe shot out of the opposite end like a comet, bounding for the sky.

I stumbled back in awe, bumping into Arkin. He wrapped his arms around me in a hug, watching Archard deliver the soul to its future.

Seconds later, Archard returned to the Transcender, lining it with his brilliance, ready to receive the next soul.

Layla? I thought.

I know, I know, she fussed. *You don't have to sugar-coat it for me, Nev. I'll stay put until we go back.*

I pulled my brows together, confused. *Go back?*

To Hell. Do what you have to do here. I won't fight you. I know what's coming, and I deserve every bit of —

Layla, I interrupted brashly, *I know you've been a massive bitch, but I can feel what's in your heart. If God can forgive my sins, yours can be absolved too. The guilt and regret I sense from you, rivals my own. Surely, that's enough.*

"I hope it's enough," I murmured to myself. I didn't want to think about what I would face when my turn for judgment came.

But..., she protested weakly.

It's time, Layla, I assured. *Thanks for your help back there.*

I angled my mouth into the Transcender and inhaled.

Wait! Not yet, Layla shouted in my head.

Closing my lips, I leaned back, waiting for her to continue.

I've been thinking. Maybe there's a way to save Gavyn. You're going to take Rhett back, right?

Nodding, I replied, *That's the plan. I'm just not sure what to do when I get him there. Here, I have this transcender thing. There, I'm not sure how to get the souls to actually stay where I put them.*

The impression she was shaking her head dismissively rolled through my mind. *They'll stick once you get them past the portal. The Devil distributes them where they belong. But, I don't think the Devil has to be Gavyn.*

Hell just wants the best candidate for its master. If you could find a way to give Rhett a physical form again…maybe, Hell will choose him. Resurrect him like it did Gavyn. Rhett is way more devious than Gavyn. I think Gavyn just had the strongest power and the darkest conscience available in its vicinity.

Two problems with that, I thought. *One, how do I get a physical form to do that? Two, what happens to Gavyn if it works?*

Layla remained silent, pondering the conflicts with me. *Well, I'm not sure about the body. I just know that Hell's energy needs a vessel to contain it in order to enact its will. As for Gavyn…I'm sure he'd agree, any fate is better than being the Devil.*

Right, I answered. Guilt and sympathy contracted around my heart for Gavyn.

Ok, I'm ready. I felt her soul reaching for the Transcender.

Repositioning my mouth against the marble rim, I filled my lungs with air and blew out.

While her spirit drifted into Archard's light, I caught her final words in my mind. *Please, get Dominic out. Tell him I love him. That I'm sorry.*

"I will," I said out loud.

Thank y – , her words cut off as the last of her soul left me.

Archard zoomed through the waves of bright colors, depositing Layla in her Heaven. A gleaming star flickered to life, promising her sins had been forgiven, and she'd rest in peace.

I gnawed on the inside of my cheek, dreading the next soul I had to say goodbye to. One occasion of losing your father was more than enough. Between losing George the first time, losing Kenet twice, and surrendering George now, I'd have done it four times.

Swallowing back the reluctance tightening my throat, I stiffened my back and my resolve.

George? His presence swept through me in a flood of awareness. Goosebumps puckered across my flesh. He was a summer breeze in my winter, warming my frosted facade.

I'm here, Nevaeh.

A tear trickled down my cheek as I appraised the vast expanse of souls waiting for my father to join them. I shuffled my feet in the grass and swiped the wetness from my face.

You ready then? I asked.

Part of me wanted him to say no. Selfishly, I wished I could keep him locked away in my soul-transporting pocket and pull him out during times I would need him in the future. Yeah, I knew it didn't work like that, but one could indulge in a little selfish thinking when facing the loss of a loved one, right?

Nevaeh, I —

"Stop," the command thundered from the gates, interrupting George's statement.

I turned toward the luminescent fence line. The bars shifted quickly, closing behind the angel heading our direction.

Malach ate up the distance between us with long, purposeful strides. He hefted a man over his shoulder where he'd carried Jacan when entering the gates. This man was slightly plump, though, and not as tall as Jacan.

My gaze traced along worn soles of familiar black tennis shoes, a sliver of gray tube socks, and dark-blue denim cuffed at the ankles. We never could find him a pair of jeans that fit right.

The Archangel slowed to a stop. He grinned, taking in my confused expression. He lowered to one knee, gently laying the body on the ground at my feet. The gesture reminded me of a cat bringing a dead bird to its owner's doorstep, seeking praise for the present it caught.

"I came baring gifts," he said, lifting his brows to elicit a response from me.

"Wha...," was all I managed. I was too afraid to hear the explanation for his gift.

"Vanna. She said He was giving George his life back." Malach's hand slid down George's arm and moved the corpse's fist to rest on his rounded belly.

I gulped down the proposal he made, trying to accept it as truth, but seriously doubting what my ears heard. Blinking hard a few times, I realized that it truly was George's body laying at my feet, and he didn't look the least bit decomposed. I searched for the faintest gray in his skin — hell, he was paler in life than he was in death. His graying hair held a shine that made him look like he was healthy and just sleeping.

"I'm sorry," I whispered around a croak. Clearing my throat, I tried again. "I'm sorry, I don't think I heard you right."

Before I could ask him to verify what the fuck he said, Malach jumped in. "You heard me, Nevaeh. Father is giving you a gift. One to help mend the pain his other gift has caused you." He shifted his other leg under him, sitting on his calves. His peridot eyes swept over George's length. "He's giving you a onetime chance to restore a soul. Put it back where it belongs, Nev."

My lips quivered. My tongue tied in a knot. I was too damn stunned to process a clear thought.

God was giving me back the thing Rhett had taken from me months ago, hurling me down this never-ending drain of pain.

"Nevaeh?" Malach prompted. "You understand what an amazingly rare opportunity this is, right?"

I nodded, mindlessly staring down at George. As the reality of my chance set in, my heart sped up, gratitude and elation blooming in its chambers.

George —

No, Nevaeh, he interrupted in a sympathetic tone.

"What?" I breathed.

No, he repeated, firmer this time. *This was always my fate, girl.*

But —

This is how it's s'posed ta be.

George, I need you, I pleaded.

How much time could I possibly have left, Nev? I'm an old man. Been through a lot. I made peace with my death. You should too.

My shoulders sagged, the sharp stab of grief taking my breath away.

Pressing my palms into my temples, I squeezed my head to relieve the impending headache and sorrow. "I can't do this without you," I bemoaned.

You already have. Let me go, Nevaeh. Let me find my Bonnie and Anna in those stars.

I remained silent, knowing what he requested was more than fair. He'd paid more than his dues in Hell. He deserved to be with his family. My need to keep him close for what...another decade, maybe...was greedy. Who was I to keep him from his family just so I could steal a few more years with him.

I didn't want that for George.

Oh, old man, I thought, wiping tears away on my sleeve, *I'm gonna miss you.*

I scanned the array of souls sparkling above, forcing my tears to dry with a sniffle. Peace settled my mourning heart. He'd be happy up there.

Glancing down at his body, I said, *At least, I'll be able to give you a proper burial, now.*

Don't, he answered. *You need a vessel to put that Devil back in Hell? Take mine.*

My eyes flicked up to Malach's then to Arkin's.

"What?" Arkin asked. He raised his brows in bewilderment, wrinkling the skin on his forehead.

It was easy to forget, at times, that I was the only one hearing the voices in my head. "He...," I could barely say the words. It seemed like I was disrespecting George for even going along with it. How could I damn a soul using the body of a man I loved so dearly? Bowing my head, I started again. "George wants me to use his body to trap Rhett in Hell."

The two angels observed each other thoughtfully, mulling the idea over in their heads.

Arkin shrugged. "It could work."

"Could?" I huffed. "I need something more than 'could.' Layla told me Hell just needed a physical form to harness its energy. But, I need to be pretty damn sure with this."

Malach planted his hands on his muscular thighs and pushed himself up. One hand rubbed his jaw, while the other hand perched on his right hip. He paced in a slow circled. "He's right. It should work. You've got one shot with this, though, Nevaeh. Father gave you the power to use your gift in reverse one—"

"One time. Yes, I got that," I snapped.

Arkin patted my back then smoothed a path between my shoulder blades. "I've got faith in ya, cupcake."

A thought suddenly occurred to me. I narrowed my eyes at Malach, folding my arms over my middle. "Do you think He planned it this way? I mean, if God knows everything, do you think this was all in His grand scheme? To give me back George, but really just give me his body to take care of Rhett?"

Malach chuckled at my scattered questions. "Would it matter? George was given the opportunity, and he did what he felt was right with it. If he had chosen to accept the gift, you'd have each other back, which would've been a win. Instead, he opted to be with his family in the Heavens and sacrifice his body for an honorable purpose that will make him a legend among the angels. Also, a win. Father may have known how it was going to go, but He still allowed George the choice, Nev. That's what it's all about. Free will."

I flung my hands down at my sides, expelling an irritated breath. I hated when Malach made sense.

Rolling my eyes at him, I marched over to the Transcender. I drew in a cleansing breath and redirected my emotions. "Are you ready, George?"

Yeah, baby girl. I been ready fer this a long time. Just didn't know I'd be given the blessing.

"I love you. Always will."

Love you too, kid. Always have.

Archard's glow flared, welcoming George's soul into his fold as I exhaled my father's spirit.

My eyes shot upward, following the shooting star zooming to be with the other souls.

After a moment of silence, Malach spoke. "I have one more offering."

I twisted to see the Archangel skirting George's body to stand beside Arkin.

Arkin's posture stiffened when he looked down at the hand Malach held out toward him. Malach's palm radiated a soft buttery-gold light.

"Is that...?" Arkin's wide eyes beamed at Malach's satisfied expression.

"I'm honored to give this back to you, brother." He inched his hand farther out, gesturing for Arkin to take it.

Arkin didn't reach for Malach's gift. Instead, he lifted his hand to the nape of his neck and rubbed. His face contorted, portraying the argument he was having with himself internally, as he concentrated on Malach's palm.

I stepped closer to the angels, wondering what Malach was giving him back.

"Yeah, I think I'll pass," Arkin finally said, backing away from Malach.

Malach's happy expression fell. "Wait a damn second." His hand lowered a bit. "You're really going to turn this down?"

Arkin made a sucking sound through his teeth, his lip curling up in a polite smile. "I think I am."

I butted in. "What is it? What's he turning down?"

Malach laughed, turning to the side. His face turned up to the sky, exasperated. "I can't believe it."

"What's happening?" I shifted my gaze between the two beings.

"I'm turning down my Holiness," Arkin admitted.

I giggled in disbelief. "I must be hearing things again. It sounded like you were denying the thing that makes you an Angel of Heaven."

"Nope. You're hearing pretty well. But, cupcake…I'm an Angel of Heaven no matter what." He glanced back longingly at the small portal churning above the Earthly realm. "Besides, I believe Father will understand."

"Oh, He'll understand alright. He knows what an idiot you are," Malach scoffed.

I canted my head to the side, seeing Arkin through a different light. "Love. You're doing it for love, aren't you?"

He shrugged, his wings bobbing with his movement. "She means more to me than the power to cross that portal." He smirked, winking at me. "You'll be bringing me back here one day anyway."

A smile tugged at my mouth. He was so free-spirited, not confined by perimeters of what was expected of him. "Right," I assured.

"Plus, with Archard gone, you'll need someone to look after you. I'll be your Guardian, Nevaeh." His eyes warmed, relaying the brotherly love he felt for me. "If you'll have me."

I slammed into him, throwing my arms around his neck and nuzzling my cheek into his chest. He wrapped his big arms around me.

"Thank you," I whispered.

"Well, shit," Malach groaned behind me. Seconds later, he encircled his arms around the both of us, smushing me against Arkin harder.

"Ok, ok. I have some more business to tend to." I shoved the two massive angels away and wiggled free from the group hug.

"Malach, you wanna carry George? I'll hold onto Arkin."

Malach hoisted George up, cradling him in his arms. "Let's finish this."

I turned, considering the iridescent swirls of Heaven's gates, the endless starry sky, the welcoming colors of God's love, and the Soul Transcender, where my angel, and part of my heart, now resided. Months ago, I was just a homeless girl, living day to day. I never imagined I'd be at God's door.

Arkin pulled me into his side, coaxing me to hold on for the ride. "You'll be back soon enough, Nev. You'll have a lifetime of bringing souls here. I promise. There's too many good people, you won't be able to stay away for long."

He flexed his wings, hauling me upwards then down into the portal after Malach.

NEVAEH

CHAPTER THIRTY-ONE

BRING GEORGE

The ruckus in the room shook me as we descended from the Heaven portal. All my senses shot into high-alert.

Twenty or so demon corpses were scattered along the factory floor. Three Guardians lay in puddles of blood, getting trampled in the midst of ongoing battles. Thankfully, the Hell portal's smoldering edges were holding steady, occupying only a quarter of the training room, now.

The shrill sound of Maggie screaming obscenities at the Crucio cornering her against a wall opposite us caught both mine and Arkin's attention.

He tucked his wings in close, speeding up our landing. "You good?" he shouted, his eyes locked on Maggie after depositing me safely on the ground.

"Yeah," I responded, but Arkin was already heading for the demon crowding his girl.

Scouring the training room, I found Malach making a beeline for Gavyn. Hope bloomed in my chest. Hope that I'd be able to save Gavyn from the damnation dragging his soul into the undertow. "I'll be just fine," I said to myself, setting off to join Malach.

I opened my mouth, allowing my beast her freedom. She poured through my lips, hungry to do my bidding. The storm clouds hovered around me, crackling with *my* power, *my* lightning.

This was *my* show now.

Holding out my hands, I thrust my fingers straight and willed her to attack the demons. The sharp cracking whips of electricity surged from my core, zapping every demon in the room.

The foul odor of burning sulfur and singed flesh wafted into the air.

I discharged another batch of lightning, keeping the flow circuiting until the sweet sound of bodies dropping rang in my ears.

The grunts and groans of war diminished with the number of demons. My storm's raging winds became the dominating sound.

Gavyn hunched, moving in a careful circle around Malach. The Arch had George's corpse draped over his shoulder.

I pressed the heel of my boot down on the clumped, blood-chain tethering Gavyn to Hell.

His back bowed in pain. His face morphed into a strained grimace. Gavyn's hands shot up to the collar around his neck, clawing at the unforgiving leash.

"Hello, Gavyn," I greeted in a calm tone.

Lifting my heel from his leash, I advanced on him. My heart contracted tight when I came face to face with the new master of Hell.

I'd give anything to get him back...the Gavyn this lost soul used to be. He was so far from where he once was. I couldn't find even a hint of the loving, considerate man in this Gavyn's eyes. Black lines of Hell's poison branched around his dark olive-green irises, much like they had on Rhett's arms. Much like I'd felt vining around my soul not too long ago.

I scrutinized the harsh ridges of his cheekbones and jaw, the angry flare of his nostrils, his gnashing teeth...the spittle on his dry lips.

His furious gaze consumed me, while I contemplated how I could free him.

"Where did you go?" I breathed.

Gavyn's narrowed eyes widened then darted down to the floor, avoiding my judgement.

Without thinking, I raised a hand and cupped his cheek.

"Nevaeh," Malach warned.

I glanced over my shoulder, giving him a nod that hopefully conveyed I knew what I was doing.

Gavyn's hand clenched around my wrist and yanked me into him. His arms wrapped around me, tightening to an uncomfortable pressure. My feet dragged along the floor as he pulled me toward Hell.

Well, this was not really part of my plan, but I was going back one way or another. I stopped struggling and yelled at Malach. "Bring George."

The tell-tale pull of the portal latched onto me, helping Gavyn transport me from one realm to the next.

"Nev," Malach called in a rough voice. Worry lines etched his forehead. "Fuuuuck."

As Gavyn and I breached the opening, I watched the Archangel gather his courage, tightening his grip on George, then barrel toward the portal after me.

HAVEN CAGE

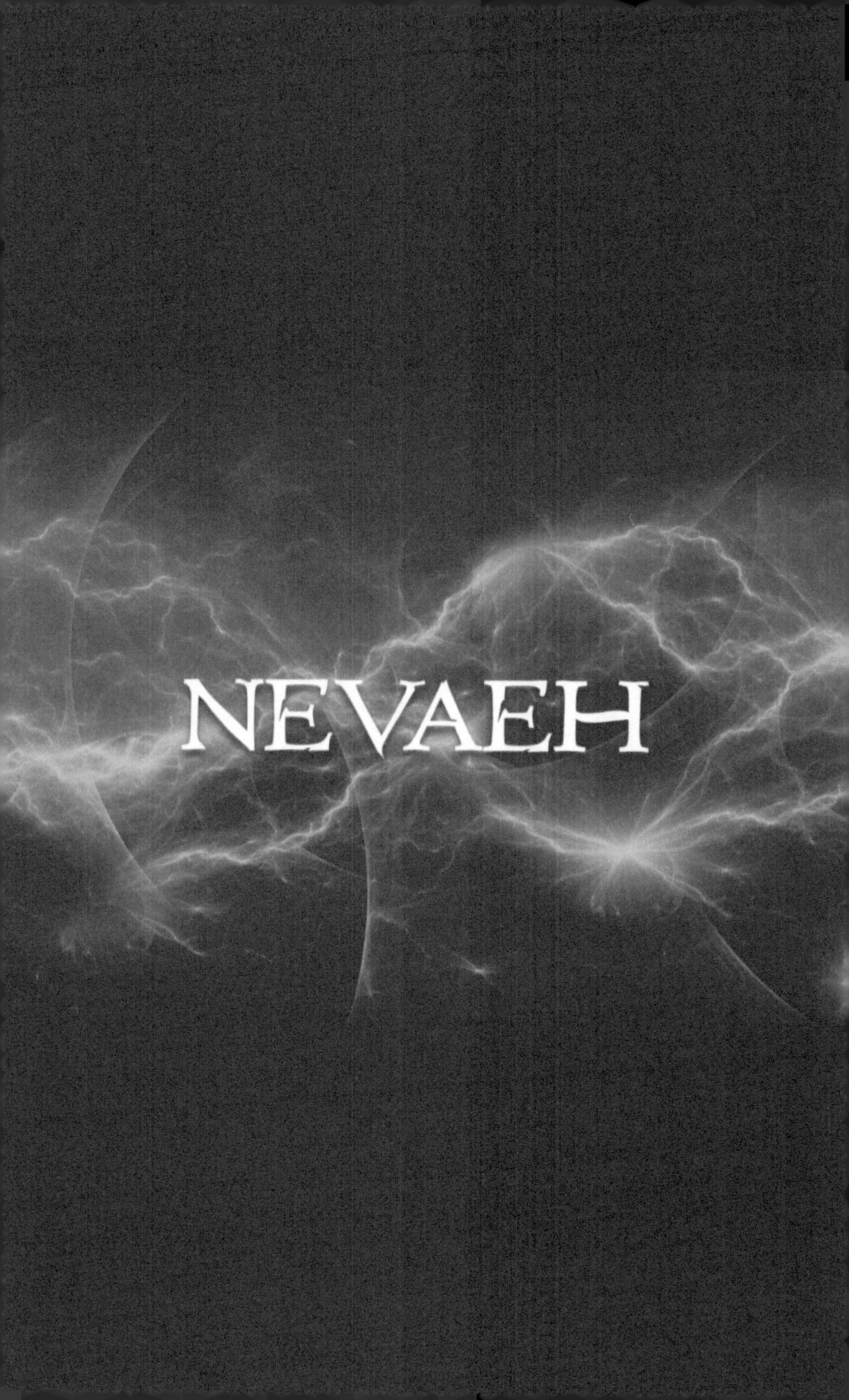
NEVAEH

CHAPTER THIRTY-TWO

Back In His Rightful Place

"Gavyn, let me go." I scraped his forearms, prying against his hold on my waist.

He merely grunted with annoyance, ignoring the tiny rivulets of blood I drew, and lugged me deeper into the depths of the Underworld.

"Listen, I can free you," I gritted.

He laughed humorlessly. "I used to think you might be able to, but I'm pretty sure it's too late."

"I have Bron's soul inside me. We've got a plan. Let me go, and I'll prove it to you."

"Not gonna happen. I've got to get to him."

A whizzing sound jetted past my left ear. Gavyn stilled. His arm loosened around my middle before he toppled into the rocky wall next to us.

I didn't wait to see what happened next. All I knew was Gavyn was knocked for a loop, and I was free.

Hurriedly, I brushed my fingers along his chest, firing a low voltage shock to incapacitate him. He convulsed for a second, then dropped to the dirt.

Leaning over him, I check for a pulse on his jugular. His dark heart was still beating. For how long, I wasn't sure.

"Is he dead?" Malach asked, concerned.

Noticing a baseball-sized rock speckled with blood lying next to Gavyn's shoulder, I thanked God for Malach's keen ability to improvise with weapons. I was two seconds from calling my beast in, but Malach's rock was less dramatic and did the job well.

"Not yet." I straightened, helping the angel prop George's body on the wall next to Gavyn. "Glad you made it through ok."

His mouth quirked up in a sarcastic smile. "Gee, thanks. Aside from the fact if felt like my skin was being ripped off in thin strips, and my insides were being barbecued, it was a piece of cake. Oh, then there was the petty little detail of sacrificing some of my Holiness to break the demon barrier, but that was no sweat too."

"I'm sorry, but we had some last-minute plan changes." I nudged my chin toward Gavyn. "I didn't realize he was going to kidnap me."

"Maybe if you weren't being so cocky, and watched what your enemy was doing, you could have brought George yourself."

"I think you'll live," I grumbled.

"We'll see when I try to make it out of here."

A blood-curdling scream echoed through the tunnel. I glanced toward the sound, my stomach wrenching from a rush of haunting memories that accompanied the shriek. "Let's get this done."

"Here?" Malach scoped both ends of the dim corridor. "We should probably find somewhere better-guarded from the bazillion demons wandering around, don't you think?"

"These tunnels go on forever, and I'm not exactly sure where in Hell we are. If we try to find a better place, we could end up in a much less favorable location. Trust me, there are plenty of those. Just keep a look out. They'll only come from two directions."

Malach pressed his lips together, unsheathing his sword. "I see that." He tipped his head toward an Animus creeping up on us.

The Archangel stretched his wings out, capturing what dank air current he could in this wasteland, and leaped for the demon. Malach landed, stabbing his blade into the demon's black, sunken eye. It screeched out a warning before Malach twisted the sword, jamming it deeper into the fiend's skull. The demon quieted and slumped to the dirt.

"I suggest you get started, Nev. They'll be here in droves before too long."

I quickly straddled George's legs and tilted his head back. Curling one hand around the vessel's chin, I urged its mouth open.

"This can't be much different than the Transcender, right?" I babbled to myself.

"Come on, Nevaeh," Malach urged. He engaged his warrior's stance, his shoulders broadening, knees bending, and his face fierce. He lunged, killing another intruding demon.

I leaned down, lining my lips up to what used to be George's.

Rhett, you fucker, I know you're in there, I thought, scavenging that deep, dark, lonely place where he kept me imprisoned inside myself.

From now on, I would stash all the damned souls there.

The cold chill of wickedness and desperation met my senses. *It's time to pay up,* I scorned.

I exhaled into the corpse's mouth. A defiant wisp of Rhett's essence slithered passed my teeth. Inhaling and exhaling a second time, I drudged up every bit of his soul, scraping it from my depths like gum from my shoe.

The fallen angel's vapors filled George's mouth.

I sealed my lips on the vessel's and blew out one last forceful breath to stuff him down farther.

Sitting back on George's knees, I watched for signs of reanimation.

Nothing.

Malach sliced the head off a Crucio demon barging in from my left. "Is it done?" he asked, panting.

I lifted my shoulder in a half shrug. "I think so, but I'm not sure. We thought Gavyn was dead too, but clearly that wasn't the case."

My gaze roamed over the current Prince of Darkness. His head drooped to the side, sweaty strands of espresso-hued hair sticking to his forehead. With his eyes closed and his tense expression relaxed, Gavyn resembled a version of his former self.

Archard and I had something special. Something that surpassed boundaries of Heaven, Hell, and Earth. He'd always claim a portion of my heart, of my soul. He was my Guardian. We were bonded on a level so deep, he was stitched into the very threads of my being. Yet, I recognized the twinge in my heart when I looked at Gavyn.

It seemed like centuries ago, but there once was a time I felt something for this man too. I felt it now, and though it was much different, I still sensed the static-charge and gravity between us.

Gavyn had claimed the other part of my heart. He'd stamped his mark on my soul the minute he held my hand into this dark world. When he sacrificed himself — his faith, his dignity — to save my soul, that mark etched deeper into the tender skin of my existence.

When I was lost, I fought it, afraid of what we had both become in Hell. We shared something though. We'd been the worst versions of ourselves, seen how far our power could push us over the edge.

I couldn't refute our bond, or the relationship we were building when I first walked into Joe's Café, any more than I could refute what Archard and I had.

They were two halves of my whole.

I crawled off Rhett's new body. Huddling over Gavyn, I caressed his dirt-smudged cheek.

His eyes snapped open, fear and misery shading them in the darkest moss.

"I...," he strained, "I'm so sorry, Nev." A deep wheeze rattled his chest as he spoke. "I never meant...for this to...happen," he stammered. His teeth clenched. His lips pulled back in a snarl. "I just wanted you to...be safe."

There he was, the man I met months ago. The one who'd searched for me the night I entered my first portal. The one who offered me a life of stability and love. The one who gave himself so freely.

A black, wet spot bloomed just over his heart, tearing my attention from his pained expression. I dragged my finger over the fluid soaking his shirt to inspect it closer. He hissed in a breath.

I shoved his shirt up.

Sitting back on my feet, I stared at the line splitting open over Gavyn's breastbone. It was the very spot Archard plunged his sword.

"I guess it worked," Malach said, squatting down on the other side of Gavyn. His brows pinched together as the heaviness of the moment pushed down on us.

I knew this was a possibility. I'd almost counted on it. Hell's energy would have to leave Gavyn to possess Rhett again. That meant Gavyn might not continue to live without Hell keeping him alive, since he was dead before it resurrected him. The knowledge of what might happen didn't make it any easier to watch.

Would there be no one left for me in the end? Is it my fate to be alone in this grim voyage? George was gone. My Celata mother and demon father were dead. And Archard would never be able to see the Human realm again.

Maybe it was best. This was no life for a happy couple.

Gavyn groaned, gurgling around a pool of blood flooding his mouth.

"I hope you can forgive me, Gavyn." I frowned, wiping a trickle of red from the corner of his lips. "I just couldn't leave you here…like *that*."

He caught my hand, struggling to speak. "No need to forgive," he choked out. Gavyn gifted me with a warm smile. "I never wanted to be a monster…You are saving me…just like I knew you would."

Unable to restrain it any more, a sob burbled up from my chest. Tears streamed down my cheeks.

"Save him, Nev," he wheezed. "Save Dom."

I raised my brow, realizing Dom was stuck down here. Layla had asked me to save him too.

"Where, Gavyn? Where is he?" I asked frantically. He could've been anywhere in the endless maze of sinners. Dominic could be dead before I found him. He could be dead already.

Gavyn's eyes closed, the strain on his face washing away with unconsciousness.

I shook his shoulders, fighting to keep him awake. "Gavyn," I yelled. "Gavyn, stay with me." My head knew he was dying, knew he couldn't stay trapped in Hell's grasp, but my heart was not ready to let him go.

Malach gently wrapped his fingers around my wrist, bringing my hysterical, useless attempts to make Gavyn obey to an end.

I hid my face in my hands, weeping for Gavyn, for George, for Archard, my grandmother, my father, my mother, Layla, and Father Varga.

So many souls lost at my expense.

Gavyn's body trembled against my knee. I lowered my hands. His muscles bunched then released, repeating until the actions morphed into violent convulsions. He thrashed on the dirt, smacking his limbs and head on the hard ground.

Malach and I pinned each of his shoulders down, knowing it wouldn't matter now that he was gone. His body went rigid. His chest stretched up to the ceiling, spine lifting off the floor in a high arc.

Black, inky fluid spewed from the wound in Gavyn's chest and clumped together in oily droplets on the dirt. The substance resembled the chilling wicked waves of Sinner Sea and moved with its own volition.

It skittered across the ground in a goopy, congealed mess. Thin, spiked fingers poked out of the tarry puddle, latching onto Rhett's motionless hand. It climbed up Rhett's arm like a spider creeping in on a web-bound fly until it crested his shoulder. The thin fingers elongated, crawling up Rhett's chin. The entity pried open Rhett's mouth, forcing it to gape open in a frightful yawn. Rhett's tongue invited the glob into his throat where it disappeared into his depths.

Rhett's eyes popped open. He sucked in a loud gasp. It was George's body, but there was no trace of the George I knew remaining. I was peering into Rhett's loathsome gaze.

Satisfaction tingled along my skin. I smirked. Leaning forward, I paused an inch from his nose. "Best settle in and get comfy in there, Rhett.

With all the souls I'll be delivering to you for punishment, I'm sure we'll see plenty of each other. I'm going to make sure you stay here for the rest of my life. And when the next Soul Bearer comes? I guarantee they'll know exactly who you are." Victorious laughter erupted up from my gut.

Rhett sneered at me. He rolled over, grabbing at the wall until he managed to stand. "I'll find a way out. This is not over, Nevaeh," he sputtered, stumbling away from us.

"Don't count on it, Devil."

He vanished into the shadows of the tunnel.

"Do you think you can keep him from weaseling his way out again?" Malach asked.

I turned on my shins, the grains of earth grating through my pants. My gaze fell on what was left of Gavyn, and the victory I'd experienced moments earlier evaporated.

"The most he can do without me is breach a portal for a short period of time." I slapped my palm against the rough rock wall next to me, eyeing its jagged surface. The power in this realm was deceiving. There were few who found freedom once they entered, even if they made it past the portal. "He may be able to take a little vacay up top, but Hell's got its claws dug in deep…he won't be able to escape easily."

I raised my eyes to meet Malach's. "And, I vow, with every bit of my God-given gifts, to plant his ass so far down in this putrid soil, his roots will never see the light of day again."

Malach's lips twitched, the hint of a smile creating a small dimple in his right cheek. "Your family would be proud, Nevaeh. I know I am."

I swallowed hard, fighting the sting of tears. It meant so much for him to admit such a thing. He was an Archangel. A warrior of God. For him to be proud of me, a little street-wretch, considering all the bad I'd done, seemed impossible.

"Thanks," I replied, my voice cracking. I cleared my throat, finding my strength. "We need to find Dominic. Can you carry Gavyn?"

I ignored the pain constricting my chest. There was no time to grieve. We needed to find Layla's brother and get him out of here. I'd have to save my mourning for another day.

"I think I can do one better."

Malach splayed his hand over Gavyn's wound. Soft, golden light sparked to life, spreading out from his fingertips.

DOMINIC

CHAPTER THIRTY- THREE

Unexpected Gifts

"He's coming back. He's coming back," I repeated, drowning out the whispers in my skull.

Rocking back and forth, I sat on Gavyn's floor cross-legged. It seemed like days since Gavyn was here. I didn't know how much longer I could stay cooped up in the small room, avoiding the demons outside only to remain trapped with the demons inside.

I dug my fingers into my temples. Maybe I could scratch through the thin skin there and scrape the voices out with my nails. It wouldn't take much effort.

My face hurt from squeezing my eyes shut and grinding my teeth. They wouldn't stop. Nothing I did quieted them.

He's dead. He can't save you, they whispered in my thoughts.

They rarely lied to me. However, they often spoke in riddles that made sense in one manner yet meant something completely different.

The loneliness blanketing me said they might be right, though. It was easy enough to believe. Or was Gavyn, the man, dead, leaving behind Gavyn, the monster. The monster surely would never save me.

Knock, knock.

"Go away," I whispered to the demons on the other side of the door. They constantly rapped on the metal, trying to convince me to let them in.

"Dominic?" a new voice called.

I dropped my hands and froze, staring at the door as if I could create a peep-hole with my eyes.

"Dominic, you in there?" Another knock followed the question.

It was Nevaeh.

Had Gavyn found her? Had he come back for me?

Or had Nevaeh's evil consumed her?

I scanned over the room, devoid of life aside from me. There was no way I could stay a prisoner in here any longer.

Unfolding my legs, I stood. I inched toward her voice.

"Where's Gavyn?" I pressed my ear against the cold metal.

"Oh, thank God," Nevaeh sighed. "Open the door, Dominic."

I shook my head, even though she couldn't see me. "Gavyn said not to answer unless it was him. Where is he?"

"I'm here, man. You can let us in," Gavyn answered.

I released the breath I'd been holding to brace for the news that he was dead.

Wrenching back the lever I'd locked after Gavyn left, I disengaged the bolt and yanked on the knob.

Gavyn stood, smiling, in the center of the doorway. Nevaeh and an angel stood on either side of him.

I threw myself into Gavyn, hugging him tight.

He hooked his arms around me, pulling me in tighter. "You ready to go home?" he asked. His hot breath ruffled my hair, warming the chill of loneliness in my bones.

I nodded emphatically, leaning away to rid an escaping tear with my sleeve.

"Come on, then." He guided me across the threshold.

"Wait. We can't leave yet." I sprinted down the tunnel.

"Dominic," Gavyn called after me.

The trio set into motion, chasing me. Their feet pounded close behind, indicating I hadn't lost them. "This way," I yelled, turning a corner.

I led them to a secret alcove I'd covered by rolling boulders in front of it. After hours of watching the spot, I learned the demons paid these secluded hiding areas little attention most times.

"Here," I said, pointing to a stone as tall as I was.

The angel narrowed his eyes at me, gauging my intentions. He shook his head, revealing his trepidation, but shoved the boulder aside anyway.

Gavyn stepped forward to inspect the dark space, but I captured his wrist. He stopped, looking back at me with a puzzled expression on his face.

"She has to do it," I directed, pointing at Nevaeh.

"Okay," she agreed, hesitantly. Nevaeh nodded at the angel, gesturing he step out of her way. "I'll be alright, Malach."

She snapped her fingers, bringing forth a spark of purple light that crackled and spewed like a sparkler from her fingertip. Holding out her hand, she entered the crevice, lighting the way with her power.

A sharp gasp echoed off the rocks. Her head poked out of the opening, and she grinned at me. A tear fell from her beautiful eyes, her graciousness shining bright. "Thank you."

She disappeared into the sliver, then backed out of it, dragging a body with her.

"My God," Malach exclaimed, his brows jumping high.

"It's your mother? You look like her," I said, comparing Nevaeh's high cheekbones and dark curls to the bloodied corpse at her feet.

Nevaeh's teeth caught her lower lip, preventing the frown trying to take over. She nodded sullenly before going into the alcove once more.

"And this is my other father. I was lucky enough to have two." She gazed up at Gavyn and Malach, the three of them sharing a knowing glance.

"I saw them in the skin-room. I hid them here in case you came back. Didn't want the demons defiling them. Something kept telling me they didn't belong here."

Nevaeh winked at me then raised her face to the ceiling.

Was she praying?

The roar of wild winds answered my question seconds later. A dense black storm, flickering with her purple lightning bolts, rolled in around us.

Nevaeh bent over her mother. She propped the corpse's mouth open using her thumb and forefinger. Sucking in a deep breath, she pulled something from her mother's mouth, inhaling the glowing substance until it was all out.

When Nevaeh finished her mother, she moved to her father and repeated the ritual.

With another deep inhale, she swallowed the storm clouds. The dense black poured into her mouth, nose, and eyes, stowing away deep in her small frame.

It didn't seem like Nevaeh had enough room in her body to contain the storm, but, somehow, she gulped down every last wisp of it.

"Now we can go home," I said.

Nevaeh stood, giving her parents a silent goodbye. She snapped her fingers then fisted her hand. In one fluid sweep, she drew a circle of burning embers into the air.

NEVAEH

CHAPTER THIRTY-FOUR

TYING UP LOOSE ENDS

"That's it, boys. Get them as close as you can stand, I'll do the rest," I encouraged, lugging an Animus toward the portal.

The Guardians worked their tired, bruised bodies for another hour, helping me gather the demons that had breached the portals.

I rolled each one across the fiery border of Hell, returning them to their proper cage.

Would demons still escape? Sure, but I'd be there to kick their decomposed asses home.

Rhett lingered on the opposite end of the opening, watching me reverse the damage we'd caused.

As I hefted the last fiend into the Underworld, Malach came up beside me. "Looks like that's it," he panted, having thrown a good many demons into the pit as well.

"Yeah." I wiped my forearm across my brow, ridding the sweat dripping in my eyes.

Malach licked his lips and glanced over his shoulder at Gavyn. He collected abandoned angel weapons from the floor and handed them to Dominic, so he could clean the blood off before sorting them on the weapons table.

"You did the right thing, Malach. Arkin even agreed."

The Archangel's eyes wandered away from his ward, surveying the disheveled room. "I just hope Arkin doesn't resent me for giving Gavyn his Holiness one day."

I rolled my eyes, huffing out an irritated groan. "He won't. He chose his future. Arkin would much rather you save a life using something he didn't want than you hanging onto it until he changed his mind." I nudged my chin toward the couple picking up broken glass next to the door. "Maggie is all he needs to be happy. When the day comes, either me or some other Soul Bearer will take him to the Heavens to rest. For now, she's enough."

I reached out, resting my hand on his folded arms. "I, for one, can't thank you enough for bringing him back. I'm sure Dominic appreciates it too."

Malach offered a faint smile and nodded. "Guess I should get the remainder of the traitors back. Vanna is waiting."

The Guardians had succeeded in injuring, but not killing, two of the Dominions while we were gone. The third traitor lost his life to an Aether demon. One of the two alive was missing a leg and the other an eyeball, but I thought that was a fair price to pay, considering.

"Yep. It's time the chain is restored. I'm sure she's anxious to return to her sphere. We'll take care of things down here."

He hooked his hand around the back of my head and pulled me into his chest, hugging me tight. "I know you will. I have faith in you," he murmured into my hair. "Take care of him, too."

"I will." Gavyn was all I had left of the world I knew before this started. "You'll be back soon, right?" I asked, sensing the discomfort of a long goodbye in our embrace.

He let out a weary sigh. "I'll be around. You just won't see me. It's time I act like the Guardian I was supposed to be since the beginning." Stretching back to look at me, he winked.

"Aren't you gonna tell him goodbye before you go?" I glanced over the angel's shoulder at Gavyn, worried Gavyn might feel abandoned once he finds out Malach left without a word.

"There will never be a goodbye between us. He knows that."

Malach released me and marched toward the disabled Dominions. He grabbed a hand from each, then launched into the whirling mercury waters above.

With the demons back in Hell, and the Dominions on their way to sentencing, it was time to close the veils.

I held out my fist, winding it in a wide circle. The burning edges collapsed, shrinking the Hell portal in on itself. A final puff of smoke noted the closure of that particular veil.

Moving to stand beneath the Heaven portal, I realized, last time I entered it, a being with wings flew me through. How was I supposed to get souls there now?

Peering up at the mirrored surface, I felt my beast stirring behind my ribs. She was unfurling, responding to my need.

I crooked an eyebrow, debating a far-fetched possibility. Chuckling at myself for having so little faith in the unknown, especially when it came to my gifts, I settled on giving her a chance. After everything that's occurred, would it really be so hard to believe that my beast could help get me into the portal?

I opened my mouth, releasing the mass of flickering clouds. She spiraled around me from head to toe. My feet lifted off the ground, the wind and air pressure of my beast pushing me up in the same manner an updraft gave the angels flight.

She transported me through the portal, gently depositing me in front of the Transcender.

This was how it would be from now on. I'd reap the souls and deliver them to the appropriate places. I knew I'd made the decision before, but it didn't seem right that I be the one to determine a person's eternity. Who was I to make that judgement?

"It's not you who determines."

I jumped, the sudden voice startling me.

Vanna edged around me, stopping on the opposite side of the Transcender. All her eyes focused on me as she traced a finger over a crooked line on the marbled surface.

"What did you say?" I asked, confused by her statement.

"He will always determine. You merely enact for Him."

I canted my head, watching her hand curl around the lip of the urn. "But, I'm the one who sees the images of their sins and their joys. I decided not to take Ray to Hell. I decided not to take Layla to Hell. "

Vanna giggled. "You are shown what you need to see. That feeling you get in your gut? The one that told you they didn't belong in the pit of sinners, regardless of their transgressions? It is Father giving you intuition. He helps you make the decision fairly and accordingly in each case. You only have to follow your instincts."

"Oh," was all I could say in response.

Well, it was good knowing my personal feelings wouldn't get in the way of what He wanted me to do.

"Rely on your gut right now, Nevaeh. Give your mother and father the afterlife they deserve." She let her hand fall from the Transcender and offered me a delicate nod. "The chain is mended once again. I'm going home."

Vanna wandered back through a small opening in the Heavenly gates. The swirling bars closed behind her.

It was my turn to pet the Transcender, imagining myself combing my fingers through Archard's hair or running a hand over his broad chest. "I'm back, my love," I whispered to the glow radiating from the base.

The light brightened in response.

My heart skipped. It was hard to know he'd never come home with me. He was already home. But, his subtle reaction excited me. He knew when I was near. He could hear me. That would have to be enough to comfort me through the years.

"I have two souls for you. Please, take special care of them." I lined my mouth up with the opening and blew, expelling my mother first, then my father.

Archard wrapped them in his radiance and carted them away.

The new star gleaming in God's fold incited a warm, fuzzy sensation in my core. It might not have been my ideal outcome, but after Rhett and the Dominions' rebellion, I was happy that the one's I'd loved and lost were glittering up there.

They had found peace.

I strolled to the portal, calling my beast with my mind. She wrapped around me, lifting me off the ground.

As we traversed back to the Human realm, I sang.

A melody that didn't match any tone in my actual voice reverberated off my diaphragm, up my windpipe, and passed my lips.

The mystical song boomed through the air, bouncing off the Heavenly molecules and commanding the portal to close.

NEVAEH

EPILOGUE: PART I

NEW LIFE

My eyes fluttered open, waking from a dream about Archard. I bowed my back off the mattress, stretching the happy remnants of my angel away for the day.

It had been two months since he died and assumed the role of ushering souls to their Heaven for me. I saw him every day — at least, the luminous embodiment of his essence — but, I still had dreams of us together. He was always in his physical form.

I chose to believe he was sending me messages of what would have been if he hadn't died. Sometimes, he even tells me how happy he is for me.

A strip of early morning sunlight peeked through the slit in the curtains, reaching across our bed. I rolled over, spooning his bare back and hooking an arm around his middle. It was time for us both to get moving.

My chilly fingertips traced the hard ripples of his stomach, inching south. His slow, sleepy breaths hitched. His warm hand caught mine before it could travel below the covers.

"Morning," I greeted with a giggle.

He groaned, low and gravelly. "Mm. Morning. Your hands are fuckin' cold."

"I was trying to warm them up, but you stopped me," I pouted.

He twisted around under the covers, dragging them up over both of us. Strong hands curled around my back, tucking me into his chest. "We could sleep a little longer."

"No, we can't. You have to get the café prepped, and I have to take him to school before I do my thing."

His eyelids blinked open. Beautiful olive-green irises beamed back at me. "I know," Gavyn whined.

I tilted my head up, kissing him quickly. "Get a move on," I teased.

When I started to scoot away from him, he threw his leg on top of mine and rolled me under him. I wrapped my legs around his waist, welcoming his heat between my thighs.

"We've got time," he whispered. His mouth crashed into mine, his hips grinding into my pelvis. "We can do without breakfast, right?" A mischievous grin lifted his full lips.

I whimpered, unable to focus on today's tasks with his length rocking against me. He was toying with me. He knew I was weak when it came to him.

The real Gavyn came home with us the day I closed the veils. He was a bit more troubled due to memories of what he'd done, but so was I. We both had our demons to contend with, metaphorically and literally.

It took a few weeks to build up a trust and figure out who we were in the aftermath, but agreeing to live together and take care of Dominic helped us find our way back to each other.

We had accepted the darkest sides of one another and made sure they stayed locked up where they wouldn't overpower us ever again.

We kept each other sane and good.

I thanked God every day for the chance to have at least one of my loves walking beside me in this dangerous world. And, as much as I loved Archard, Gavyn had filled my heart with an abundance of desire and contentment too.

I loved him. I was *in love* with him.

"No, I...," a sigh of pleasure escaped me, "I don't need breakfast."

Gavyn nibbled on my neck, scooping his arms under my spine when I arched into him. He drew his hips back then slipped into my slick heat.

I bit my lip, reigning in the urge to scream from the shock of ecstasy undulating through my body.

Gavyn had become my everything: partner in parenting, best-friend, supporter, and lover.

He was my past and my future.

NEVAEH

EPILOGUE: PART II

MY CONTRITION

"Got your lunch money?"

"Yeah." Dominic's eyes lowered to his shoes as we pushed through the crowd of high-schoolers crowding the walkways into the school.

His anxiety was high this morning, but it was far from what it had been two months ago. We'd worked extensively with other Celatum to help him gain control on the demons invading his mind.

He thanked Gavyn and I the other morning, saying that the distracting voices used to be like a train running circles around him and, now, they were little more than a gnat buzzing in his ear. He could actually function outside of a church's sanctuary.

We enrolled him in school, making it our mission to raise him as much like a normal kid as possible.

He worried his bottom lip. His short fingernails scraped back and forth nervously over the bookbag straps looped around his shoulders.

"Did you meditate this morning?"

"I went down to the café before you guys got up. I'll be okay."

We stopped at the school door. He glanced up at the lofty, brick building, his hands squeezing the bag's straps and tugging to readjust its weight.

I bumped his arm with mine playfully, giving him my warmest smile. "You got this, kid."

"I know." One corner of his mouth quirked up. "See you tonight?"

I nodded. "See you tonight."

Dominic joined the kids stampeding through the doors. I watched him until I couldn't see his scruffy hair anymore.

Skipping down the steps in front of the school, I pulled my jacket tight around me. I plunged my hands into my pockets and fondled the rosary Dominic gave me weeks earlier. My fingers rolled over the smooth amethyst beads, soothing the everyday stress of life so I could focus better.

I had my own meditation tricks.

Besides the calming string of beads, vibrations from the Fluorite stone pronged in a silver band on my ring finger traveled up my hand. It created a dull hum that strengthened my senses and amplified my gifts.

The uneasy familiarity of trouble soured my stomach. I paused next to the Stop sign at Banks and Trade. My gut was signaling me to take a left on Banks Street.

I wasn't sure what I was walking into, but a couple of months spent learning to listen to my body, heart, and soul prepared me for anything that might come along.

I knew I'd be able to handle it, whatever it was.

This was my new routine.

I used to wake up in the mornings planning what I'd do for work that day and where our next meal would come from. Now, I woke up in Gavyn's arms, saw Dominic off to school, scoured this realm for demons to send back to Hell, and reaped human souls, delivering them to peace or punishment.

At the end of the day, if everything went without a hitch, I returned to Gavyn and Dominic to do it all over again. Precious moments of heart-felt laughs and warm embraces shared between us made enduring the gloomier parts of my world worth it.

There would always be evil seeking revenge and supremacy.

There would always be darkness.

But there would always be light too.

As long as I was alive, I'd fight to keep it shining brightly, even if it took *my* darkness to keep it that way.

I had faltered in my faith, in my trust of who I was. I experienced the devastating severance that could result from such hesitation.

And this new life?

It would be my contrition until the day I died...until the moment I was able to claim *my* star in the sky.

THE END

A NOTE

Dear Reader,

If you've made it to this letter, you've followed us through the entire, gut-wrenching, anger-inducing, love-sparking, soul-shaking tale. I want to thank you, from the bottom of my heart, for taking a chance on me and my stories.

Nevaeh bloomed from my own questions about faith and the gray area of what's right and wrong. That's what these books were all about. I hope that was clear in her trials. I hope her story came across in a manner that didn't push you into the boundaries of religion, but made you ponder spirituality in general — or the lack of. I believe everyone needs to do a good evaluation of the fabric of their soul every once in a while. After all, it's what makes us who we are. It's an important part of what helps us grow as people.

It has been a long journey with Nevaeh and her family. Though this is the end of her road, I hope she is etched into your book memory-bank, and your heart, as a beloved character. She will always be my favorite since she was my first…kind of like a first love. Nevaeh holds so many of my strengths and weaknesses that I'll never be able to fully let her go, but I hope to create more great personas like her.

Please keep in touch. I'd love to see you in my other worlds.

Love,
Haven

BOOKS BY HAVEN

The Faltering Souls Series

Falter

Nevaeh Richards thinks she has found a chance to leave her homeless life behind. When the spirit of the only father she knows is wrongfully taken to Hell, Nevaeh is hurled into a world haunted by monstrous demons, rogue Guardian angels, love that is beyond her control, and a soul-threatening choice between the inherent evil inside her and the faltering faith she is struggling to grasp.

Severance

Nevaeh has to face the overpowering gravity of her choice to save those she loves while striving for strength to fight her greatest threat—herself.

Contrition

Trial after trial, Nevaeh's loved-ones have struggled to save her from a dark destiny. The time has finally come for her to return home and join the Earth-bound angels in a war threatening to destroy the Human race. Is it really Nev who's walking the Earthly plane, though?

The Perilously Pretty Series

The Perilously Pretty Series is a compilation of wicked romance novels about badass women from all eras and walks of life.

Craving Love & Death

Most women in the '50s dream of a perfect life, pleasing their bread-winning husbands and raising happy families. Vivienne…well…she dreams of a life in which she doesn't succumb to the need to murder the men she sleeps with.

Coveting Love & Revenge

1871, high-society Savannah, Georgia.

Penniless and jaded governess, Synthia James, is trapped with her employer. When he bids their young housemaid to kill a man who threatens his business, Synthia's maternal instincts take over, and she commits the heinous deed herself.

ABOUT HAVEN CAGE

 Haven Cage lives in the Carolinas with her husband and son. After many years of dabbling with drawing, painting, and working night shift in the medical field, she decided to try her hand at writing. Unfortunately, her love for books came later in life and proved to add a healthy challenging during her writing journey.

Determined to hone her craft, though, she soaks up as much information as she can, spends her free time tapping away in her favorite local coffee shop, and keeps a good book in hand whenever possible.

What began as a hobby has grown into a way of escape and the yearning to take her journey farther, her love for writing and reading deepening along the way.

Haven loves to socialize and hear from her fans. Connect with her at the following links:

Facebook.com/HavenCage/
Instagram: Haven Cage
Pinterest: Author Haven Cage
Twitter: @HavenCage

Look for Haven on Goodreads.com and add her to your bookshelf!

You can, also, visit her website at www.authorhavencage.com. While you're there, join Haven's Groupies to receive updates, exclusive sales info, and play Haven's Puzzlers for chances to win prizes.

If you enjoyed this book, please leave a review as it is how authors succeed in the publishing world. Without the reader's love, we would be nowhere.